JUDGEMENT DAY
THE CROCKETTS' WESTERN SAGA: 7

ROBERT VAUGHAN

WOLFPACK
PUBLISHING
— EST 2013 —

WOLFPACK
PUBLISHING
— EST 2013 —

Published in the United States by Wolfpack Publishing, Las Vegas

Wolfpack Publishing
5130 S. Fort Apache Road, 215-380
Las Vegas, NV 89148

wolfpackpublishing.com

Paperback ISBN 978-1-64734-785-7
eBook ISBN 978-1-64734-784-0

JUDGEMENT DAY

Chapter One

It was fifteen years now, since Will and Gid Crockett had left Missouri. During the Civil War the two brothers rode with the Confederate raiders, William C. Quantrill and Bloody Bill Anderson. Those who fought under their black flag were called Bushwhackers, and they had fought a war within a war against men from Kansas, who were called Jayhawkers.

On the grand scheme of things, the skirmishes fought between the Bushwhackers and the Jayhawkers didn't amount to much. Names like Black Oak, Tinney's Grove, and Malta Bend, didn't resonate like Shiloh, Gettysburg, or Antietam. But a comparison of the number of men engaged show the battles between Missourians and Kansans to be among the bloodiest of the war. This almost private war took on a personal aspect that had little to do with honor and much to do with killing.

After the war was over the soldiers of the two regular armies came home, some in victory, some in defeat, but all in honor. Neighbor who had fought against neighbor put down the gun and picked up the plow. They resumed the lives they had abandoned when they marched off under the flag of their cause.

That was not the case with the Bushwhackers. They weren't allowed to enjoy the peace. Men who had ridden with Quantrill and Anderson were branded thieves and murderers. Rewards were posted for their capture, in many cases dead or alive. Most had no recourse but to leave Missouri.

What made it particularly unfair was that the Jayhawkers, who had been every bit as bloody as the Bushwhackers, did not suffer that same fate. They had been on the winning side. As a result, their crimes were considered acts of war, and to them went the spoils of victory. For when a Bushwhacker had to sell his farm at distress prices, or give it up for taxes, it often wound up in the hands of someone who had been their bitterest enemy.

Some, like the James boys and the Youngers and Daltons, believed they had no choice but to take up the outlaw trail. Others who rode with Quantrill left Missouri to start a new life. Will and Gid Crockett were among that lot. Another such man was James Patton.

As James sat at the kitchen table of his west Texas ranch, he contemplated the events of the previous fifteen years that had brought him to the present. Things were fine for him now, but it had been a long struggle to reach this point.

He had been a sergeant in Will and Gid's company of Bushwhackers, and when he returned from the war, he found that his farm had been confiscated for taxes and his wife and two small children were turned out to fend for themselves. With money borrowed from relatives, James bought a wagon and moved his family to Texas.

There, by hard work and perseverance, James had prospered. His small ranch was thriving, and as his son got older and was able to help, it grew even larger. It had turned out to be a good life.

James finished his cup of coffee and looked across the table at the woman he had married, twenty years before. Anna was sitting on the other side of the table, hulling peas.

"Tomorrow is the big day," James said. "The Fourth of July picnic. Are you ready for it?"

"Well, now, just why do you think I've been shelling all these peas?" she replied. "You don't think we could eat this much by ourselves, do you?"

James laughed. "I don't know. Eric's got a pretty big appetite."

"He gets it from his father," Anna said, as she stripped open a hull, dumped the peas into a bowl, then discarded that hull and reached for another one.

James picked up a handful of peas and began shelling them.

"You don't have to do that," Anna said. "It's woman's work."

"I eat 'em, don't I?" James said. "Won't hurt me to shell a few."

Anna reached over to put her hand on her husband's hand. "You're a good man," she said.

"It'll be good to see Will and Gid again, don't you think?" James asked. He was referring to the letter they had received a few days earlier, in which Will Crockett had said that he and Gid would be passing through on the fourth.

"I don't know, James," Anna said. "I've been worryin' some about that. To be truthful with you, I'd just as soon they not come."

James stared at Anna. "Why, Anna Patton, how can you say such a thing? They're home folks. Fact is, they are the only ones from home we've seen in all the time we've lived out here."

"I know, and when the children were younger, it never bothered me. But Eric is at that age now. I'm worried about the kind of influence Will and Gid will have on him. He thinks they are heroes."

"In my mind, they are heroes."

"But, you know what kind of life they live. There's no telling how many men they've killed."

"That may be so," James said, "but I'd wager they've never killed anyone who didn't need killing."

"It's for God to determine who needs killing, not man," Anna said.

"They've been here several times, and they've always been the perfect gentlemen. Anyway, why am I having to defend them to you? They're your cousins, not mine."

"We're not that close of kin. Their mother was my mother's first cousin, that's all," Anna said. She sighed. "But you're right, they have always been well behaved around us. And it will be good to see Missouri folk again."

"Do you miss Missouri that much, Anna?"

Anna got a pensive look, then brushed a fall of hair away from her face. "I reckon I miss the hills some," she admitted. "I like the way the fog hangs in the notches in the mornin'. I like listening to the frogs at night. And I like to see green. Everything out here is so brown."

"Maybe someday, I can take you home again," James said.

Anna smiled, and squeezed James's hand. "Don't be foolish," she said. "We are home. I've got my man, my children. What more would a woman want?"

"The day you said you'd marry me was the luckiest day of my life," James said.

Together, husband and wife finished shelling the peas. Then, when the last of them was finished, Anna put a cloth over the bowl, then stood up and stretched. "I'd better get to bed. I'm going to have to start frying chicken awfully early in the morning to get enough done for the picnic."

South of the Patton ranch by about one hour's ride, two men sat around a campfire, watching the flames lick up around the bottom of a blue metal coffeepot. Felix Alvarado was only half Mexican, but with his long, sweeping mustache, wide sombrero, and colorful serape he wore, the casual observer would be hard-pressed to find any Anglo in him until they heard him talk. He spoke both Spanish and English with equal ease.

"I don't see why we couldn't have stayed in town tonight," Alvarado said. "Carmelita was going to spend the night with me."

Charley Kellett snorted. "And what were you going to do for money?" he asked.

"I don't need any money for Carmelita," Alvarado said. "Carmelita likes me."

"Carmelita likes anyone who'll spread her legs,"

Kellett said. "Get a little money in your pocket, and you can have anyone you want."

Kellett was ten years older than Alvarado. He had a long, purple lightning-flash of a scar running through his left eye, down across his cheek, and hooking up just under his mouth, the result of a wartime encounter with a saber-wielding, Confederate cavalry officer.

"And the rancher you told me about has money?" Alvarado asked.

"Lots of money," Kellett insisted. "I've heard them talk about him. He is one of the most successful ranchers around."

"Maybe he doesn't keep it with him."

"He's got it, all right," Kellett insisted. "He rode with Quantrill. They robbed so many banks during the war, that people who rode with him don't trust them anymore. He probably has it all stuffed down inside a sock and hidden in his mattress. It'll be like taking candy from a baby." Kellett laughed and snorted. "By God, it'll be good taking money from his damn rebel hide."

"The war has been over for many years now," Alvarado said.

"Not for me, it ain't," Kellett said. "I hate ever' rebel bastard what ever forked a horse. And I reckon they all hate me."

In a small, West Texas town some seven hours farther south, Will and Gid Crockett dismounted in front of the saloon, looped their reins around a hitching rail, then went inside. As soon as they stepped through the batwing doors, Will moved to one side of the opening and Gid to the other. They stood there for just a moment studying the saloon and its customers, and seeing nothing that suggested danger, exchanged a nod then moved up to the bar.

"How's your beer?" Will asked.

"It's better than horse piss," the bartender replied, laconically.

"Sounds good enough to me," Will said.

"I didn't see a hotel when I rode in," Gid said. "You got one in this town?"

"You come in from the south, did you?" the bartender asked as he drew two mugs of beer.

"Yeah," Gid said.

"That's why you didn't see one. There ain't no hotel south of here, but go on north, 'n you'll see the Red Rooster."

"Thanks."

"Can we get supper there?" Gid asked.

"You can get supper here," the bartender asked.

"Too," Gid said.

The bartender got a confused look on his face. "Too?"

"Yeah, I'll supper here to sort of hold me over until we get to the hotel, and I'll supper there, too."

"Mister, what are you talking about, hold you over? Hell, it ain't but two blocks up the street."

"My brother has what you might call a good appetite," Will said with a little chuckle.

Five minutes later the two brothers were sitting at a table. Will was on his second beer, and Gid was eating a plate of ham and beans. One of the soiled doves approached the table. She couldn't have been more than twenty years old, and she was quite attractive, though she was already showing some of the dissipation of her profession.

"Are you two boys looking for a good time?" she asked, provocatively.

"How much does it cost?" Gid asked.

"You can go upstairs with me for a dollar."

"What's your name?"

"Dinah."

"Dinah, what if we give you a dollar just to sit and have a drink with us?" Will asked.

"Why would you want to just do that?" Dinah asked.

"You see that big horse there, wolfing down his supper?" Will said, pointing toward Gid.

"This ain't supper," Gid said without interrupting his eating. "This is just to hold me over until supper."

13

"Yeah, well, Dinah that's my little brother, and I've had to look at him for the last two weeks we've been on the trail."

"That's your 'little' brother?" Dinah asked, surprised at the appellation.

"I'm older than he is, and when we were both kids, I was bigger. He might be bigger now, but I still think of him as my little brother. And I thought it might be nice to have a pretty girl to look at, instead of staring at his ugly face."

Dinah smiled, and almost blushed. "You don't have to spend a whole dollar," she said. "Just buy me a drink. That will cost you ten cents and I'll get half of it."

After the brothers left the saloon, they rode down to the Red Rooster Hotel where they ate a good supper, then took two rooms on the second floor, overlooking the street.

It was nice, sleeping in a bed.

Chapter Two

Early the next morning at the Patton Ranch, fifteen-year-old Malinda Patton was listening to the milk squirting into the bucket as she squeezed the cow's teats. She had already gathered the eggs, and the chickens were now wandering around the yard, clucking contentedly and pecking at the ground-up corn she had scattered for them.

Today was the Fourth of July, and the whole family was going into town for the celebration. There would be a picnic at noon—her mother had been frying chicken since before sun-up—then games all afternoon. Her father and brother were entered in the team horseshoe pitching contest. They won last year and had been practicing for a month to defend their championship.

Malinda's mother was entering her special plum jelly in the jams and jelly contest, and Malinda had worked for a full year on a quilt.

That was all fun, but the thing Malinda was most looking forward to was the barn dance to be held tonight. Last week she heard that the chamber of commerce had hired a real band all the way from St. Louis to provide the music. She hoped that was true. Mr. Marcellus and the Grayson brothers, who normally supplied the music, were all right. But they were old, and didn't know any of the latest songs. It would be nice to have up-to-date music to dance to.

Her brother, Eric, seemed more excited about cousins Will and Gid coming than he was about celebrating the Fourth.

"Ain't it wonderful, us bein' kin to the Crocketts?" Eric had asked over and over. "Why, they've killed more men than anybody!"

Malinda said that scarcely seemed reason to make a hero of someone, but Eric's enthusiasm wasn't dampened.

She heard the pump handle working and, looking around, saw her brother. He was holding his head under the mouth of the pump while he worked the handle. Ice-cold, deep-well water cascaded over him, washing away the dirt and sweat from his morning chores. Walking quietly, Malinda stepped up to the pump and jerked away the towel, just as Eric reached for it.

"Malinda!" Eric said angrily. "Gimme the towel you took."

"What towel?"

"If you don't want me to dry my face on your dress, you'll give me the towel."

"Oh, you mean this towel?" Malinda said. She handed the towel to him.

"Very funny," Eric said. He took the towel then began drying his face.

"Eric, Papa won't let me ride home from the picnic with Jonah Pope. He says I'm too young."

"You are too young."

"I'm only one year younger than you are," Malinda protested.

"That don't make no difference. You're a girl."

"I'm not a girl. I'm a woman, near 'bout," Malinda said. She leaned against the split-rail fence and thrust her hip out, proudly displaying the developing curves of her young body. "You tell Papa to let me ride home from the picnic with Jonah. Papa will listen to you."

"Ha! In a pig's eye he will," Eric said. "You know Pa doesn't listen to anyone." He laid the towel back across the rail. "Come on, let's go get breakfast. I'm starved."

"All we're goin' to have is biscuits and some chicken gravy," Malinda said. "Mama's been frying chicken all morning."

"That's good enough for me," Eric said.

Brother and sister walked back up the path to the

house, following the aroma of fried chicken. Eric pushed the door open, then came to a complete halt, his eyes wide with confusion. His mother and father were both in the middle of the floor, tied to kitchen chairs. They tried to shout warnings but their shouts came out as squeaks because both were gagged.

"Ma! Pa!" Eric shouted, starting toward his father.

"That's far enough, boy," a voice said. Two armed men stepped out of the pantry. One had a long, purple scar running through his left eye, down across his cheek, and hooking up just under his mouth. The other was medium-sized and dark complexioned, with a long mustache. Both were eating chicken.

"I know who you are. You're Kansas Charley Kellett!" Eric gasped, recognizing the man with the scar.

"What about that, Charley? The boy knows your name." The one with the mustache said.

"That don't matter none," Charley said. "The boy ain't needed."

Charley pointed his gun at Eric and pulled the trigger. The gun roared. A wicked flash of flame jumped from the barrel and a cloud of smoke billowed out over the table. The bullet hit Eric in the forehead, then burst out from the back of his head, carrying with it bits of bone, skin, and brain matter. Heavy drops of blood splattered from Eric's wound onto Malinda's face and fanned out onto the bodice of her dress.

"Eric!" Malinda screamed, as her brother, already dead, fell to the floor. She dropped to her knees beside him and put her hands on his face, trying desperately to deny what she was seeing with her eyes.

Suddenly James managed to work himself free from the ropes, and he jumped up from his chair. His move was so quick and unexpected, that he caught Kellett by surprise. James knocked him back and began wrestling with him for the gun.

"Alvarado! Get this son of a bitch off me!" Kellett screamed.

Moving quickly, Alvarado stepped over to the two struggling men. He stuck his gun into James's side, then, at point-blank range, pulled the trigger. As James was going down, Alvarado and then Kellett shot him again.

"We shouldn't of killed the son of a bitch," Alvarado said. "Now, we'll never learn where he keeps his money."

"We'll ask her."

Kellett removed Anna's gag. She had just seen her son and husband murdered before her eyes and was in a state of shock.

"Where's the money?" Kellett asked.

"Money? What money?" Anna replied in a confused voice. "I don't know what money you are talking about."

"Don't lie to me, woman. A ranch like this? You've

got to have money around, somewhere."

"We keep our money in the bank."

"You're lying!" Kellett said. He slapped her.

"No!" Malinda shouted. "Don't hit her again. I'll show you where the money is."

"Malinda, what are you talking about? There is no money except the money that's in the bank."

"What about the money papa buried under the tree, at the south end of the ranch?" Malinda asked.

"The south end of the ranch?" Anna replied, her voice showing her confusion.

"You know, the money he buried when cousins Will and Gid were here?"

Anna realized then what Malinda had in mind. She was going to lead the two men south, in the direction from which Will and Gid Crockett would be coming. She was taking a chance that Will and Gid would be coming at just the right moment. But no...that was too big a chance. They probably wouldn't get here until mid-afternoon.

"Malinda, no, don't do this," Anna said.

"Take care of her," Kellett growled, and Alvarado raised his gun and cocked it.

"No!" Malinda shouted. "If you hurt her, I'll never tell you where the money is. Leave her alone."

Alvarado looked over at Kellett. Kellett thought

about it for a moment, then motioned with his hand. "Take care of her," he said again.

Alvarado's gun roared, and Anna slumped in the chair, dead.

"No!" Malinda shouted.

Kellett looked at Malinda. "All right, girl, lead us to the money, or you're next."

There was no money, but Malinda led them south, hoping they would run into Will and Gid, not so much to save her life, as to avenge the killing of her mother, father, and brother.

Chapter Three

Malinda had no way of knowing that Will and Gid Crockett were still twenty miles away at that moment. They had stopped at a stagecoach way station to buy themselves a meal, feed and water their mounts, and fill their canteens.

"Did you tell Fanny Sue that we would be back next week?" Gid asked, as he forked up a large bite of biscuit and gravy.

"No," Will said. "Why?"

"Lizzie insisted that you told her that."

Will laughed. "That's just Lizzie talking. She's trying to get you to come back, that's all," he said as he began rolling a cigarette.

"Yeah, that's what I figured. You want the rest of that biscuit?" Gid asked, pointing to the half-eaten biscuit remaining on Will's plate.

Will handed the biscuit to his brother. "I wouldn't

think of depriving you."

"Well, I mean, if you don't want it," Gid said.

"You better save some room for the food at the picnic tonight," Will said. "I'll bet Anna is making a couple of her cherry pies. And you know she's frying chicken."

"Yeah, she does fry some good chicken," Gid said. "Too bad I didn't think about marrying her before James did."

"She's our cousin, for crying out loud. How could you marry her?"

"She's not 'ny closer kin to us than Zee is to Jesse, and they got married."

"Yeah, well, if you ask me, I always did think Jesse James was a little touched in the head."

The proprietor called to them from behind the counter. "You boys want 'ny more coffee? No charge for it, I need to get rid of this, 'cause I'm 'bout to make some fresh."

"Yeah, thanks," Will said. He took his and Gid's cups over to the counter. As the coffee was being poured, he happened to see a folded-up newspaper lying there. A name on the front page caught his eye, and he reached for it.

"This paper for sale?"

"Somebody left it," the proprietor said. "You can have it, if you want. It's a couple of weeks old."

Will nodded his appreciation, then returned to the table. He handed one of the cups of coffee to Gid.

"What's got you so interested?" Gid asked, taking a sip.

"This paper says Kansas Charley Kellett's been seen in the area."

"That's right," the proprietor said, overhearing them. "They say he's been seen two or three times."

"The son of a bitch rode with Otto Hoffman, didn't he?" Gid asked.

"That he did, little brother. That he did."

It was 1861. Will and Gid Crockett, who were just returning home from a business trip for their father, stopped at the gate that led onto the Crockett farm and looked at the sign:

CROCKETT FARM

Established, 1835

"The truth is, all might be free if they valued
FREEDOM AND DEFENDED IT AS THEY
OUGHT."

SAMUEL ADAMS

A grasshopper was clinging to the faded lettering and a clump of weeds had grown up in front of the sign. Will dismounted and pulled the weeds so that the sign was clearly visible.

"I thought Pa told you to re-paint this sign," Will said.

"I thought he told you."

Will tossed the weeds aside, then brushed the dirt off his hands. He tilted his head to one side and squinted. "It's not all that bad, is it? I mean, you can still read it."

"I can read it," Gid said. "Course, I could read it even if the words weren't there. Pa used to bring me out here and read it to me. It's the first thing I ever learned to read."

Will laughed as he remounted. "You weren't reading it, Little Brother, you were memorizing it."

The two brothers rode through the gate and started up the long road. Although they were back on their own farm, they wouldn't be able to actually see the house until they topped the hill. Their horses frightened a rabbit, which bounded down the lane in front of them for several feet before darting off into the safety of the tall grass.

Gid sniffed the air. "Pa must've been burnin' some brush. I can smell it."

"Yeah," Will agreed. "I can smell it, too."

They reached the crest of the hill then and looked down where the house, barn, and other outbuildings should be. But there were no buildings there. Instead there were several blackened piles of burned-out rubble ... all that remained of what had been the barn, smokehouse, outhouse, and house. Two lonely brick chimneys marked each end of what had been the house and, from the charred skeletal remains, wisps of smoke still curled up into the bright blue sky.

Their farm had been burned, their father murdered, and their mother, murdered, and raped by a gang of cutthroats riding for Otto Hoffman under the banner of the Jayhawkers. It had been that incident that set the brothers to riding for Quantrill. Over the course of the war, they caught up, not only with Hoffman, but with the specific individuals who had killed their father and raped and killed their mother. The boys had extracted their retribution.

Since the war they had learned the names of every man who had ridden with Hoffman on that night. Most were dead, but some were still alive. Kansas Charley Kellett was one of them.

"Gid? You all right?" Will asked.

Gid blinked, coming back from his memories. "Yeah," Gid said. "Yeah, I'm all right. But I'm going to be more than all right when we finally catch up with that son of a bitch."

They were four hours from the way station. As they rode across the open range, the metal bits jangled against the horses' teeth, the horses' hooves clattered on the hard rock, and the leather saddles creaked beneath them.

Their boots were dusty and well worn, the metal of their spurs, dull with time. Both men wore Colt .44s at their hips and carried Winchester .44-40s in their saddle sheaths.

"Damn, I didn't remember James's place being this far," Gid said.

Will chuckled. "You say this every time we come."

"Well, hell, it's true, every time," Gid replied. He saw something out of the corner of his eye, then turned in his saddle for a better look.

"Will," he said. "Take a look." He nodded toward the mesa.

Will looked in the direction Gid had indicated. There, circling in the sky, were several buzzards.

"Something's dying," Will said.

"Or already dead."

"Rabbit? Coyote?" Will suggested.

Gid shook his head. "Don't think so. I think it's bigger'n that."

"We'd better check it out."

The girl's nude body was blackened and swollen in the sun. She had stab wounds all over her body and one of her breasts had been hacked away. It was as brutal and senseless a murder as either of the brothers had ever encountered, and during the war they had seen more than their share of brutal killings.

"My God," Will said. "That's James's girl! That's Malinda."

The two brothers dismounted and studied not only the corpse, but the ground around it.

"We're in luck here," Gid said, pointing to the ground. "There are two of them, and one of the horses is wearing a crooked shoe. See how the end turns in, there?"

"Yeah," Will said. He looked toward the distant western horizon, in the direction the riders had gone. "I wish we could start out after them now."

"Why can't we? We need to get on them, before the trail gets cold."

Will shook his head. "No. We need to get this girl back to her mama and daddy. Besides, if it doesn't rain, the trail will still be here."

It was a solemn Fourth of July celebration, followed the next day by an even more solemn funeral for James, Anna, Eric, and Malinda Patton.

"Did you boys see any sign, anything that would give us a lead?" the sheriff asked Will and Gid.

"Not a thing," Will replied. "The ground was like solid rock. No telling which way they went."

Gid looked at Will in surprise, but didn't say anything.

"I'm pretty sure that the men we are looking for

are Kansas Charley Kellett, and Felix Alvarado. Have you ever heard of 'em?"

"I've heard of Kellett, but not Alvarado."

"Yes, well, they've been seen in the area and they are the kinds of sons of bitches who would do something like this.

"You boys going to join the posse tomorrow?" the sheriff asked. "I reckon you will be, seein' as you were friends of James."

"If you don't mind, Sheriff, I think my brother and I could be more help by going out on our own to see if we can pick up a trail. If we find anything, we'll get back to you."

The sheriff stroked his chin for a moment or two. It was obvious he didn't quite believe Will. Then he went over to his desk and opened the drawer. He pulled out a couple of badges and handed them to Gid and Will.

"I don't know what you boys have in mind," he said. "But maybe I should make you my deputies. Most of the other counties in Texas will recognize them... it'll give you some authority ... not much, but maybe just enough to keep you out of trouble."

"Thanks," Will said. He took the badge, but he didn't pin it on. Instead, he dropped it into his shirt pocket. Gid did the same.

"Remember," the sheriff said as they left his office.

"If you find anything ... get word back to the posse."

"How will we find the posse?" Will asked.

"If you had a gut feeling for where the murderers were headed for, what would that be?" the sheriff asked.

Will paused for a moment. "I'd say they were headed west." He knew that was exactly where they were going, but he didn't want company when he and Gid started after them. He knew, also, that the sheriff knew he didn't want company, so he was taking a chance that the sheriff wouldn't believe him.

"You think they are headed west, do you?"

"That's what I think," Will said.

The sheriff stared at Will, then he smiled. "Well, I'll tell you what. I know that you an' your brother want to go off on your own, so I'm figurin', there's no way you're goin' to tell me the truth. So, I got me a gut feeling of my own. And my gut feeling says they headed south."

"Could be they went that way," Will agreed.

The sheriff laughed. "You got to be pretty quick to put one over on me." He looked out the front window at the group of men who were beginning to drift over to sign up for the posse. There were cowboys, dray men, a couple of farmers, and more than one bar-fly, signing on for the dollar per day they would get when it was all over. "Hell, the truth is, I can't blame you," he added. "If I didn't have to, there's no way on God's green earth I would take this bunch of outcasts and rabble with me." He looked back at Will and Gid. "Good luck, boys," he said.

Will and Gid had crossed into New Mexico the day before. This wasn't new ground for them. They had been in this part of the country several times over the last couple of years, and actually knew it quite well. It was a pleasant surprise to them when they realized that the man they now knew was Kansas Charley Kellett, was leading them this way.

Gid stopped, then dismounted and unhooked his canteen. He took a swallow, then poured some water into his hat and held it in front of his horse. The horse drank thirstily, though the small amount of water did little to slake the animal's thirst. The horse began nuzzling Gid for more.

"That little dab of water didn't do anything but make it worse for the poor critter," Will said.

"You're probably right," Gid answered quietly. "But I had to do something. I can't stand to see him suffer so."

"We'll reach the monastery before nightfall, and there will be water there."

"Yeah. And it'll be good to see Padre Francisco again," Gid said. "I'm anxious for a rematch at checkers.

I've got a couple of moves in mind that he won't catch on to."

Will laughed. "As I recall, that's what you said last time we were through here, and he beat you pretty good."

"Yeah, he did, didn't he? I'm glad he's a religious sort of guy and doesn't bet on his games. If he did, my horse wouldn't be thirsty now, 'cause the good padre would own it."

Chapter Four

The monastery they were discussing stood alone in the desert, a testament to the faith that God would provide for the righteous, even in conditions as harsh as this. According to records kept on file in the monastery, it had been built by the Spanish nearly two hundred years earlier. There were no natural sources of food or water. The monastery garden was supported by irrigation, the water for which was brought in by the barrelful in small, mule-drawn carts, from a not always dependable river, twelve miles to the East.

Except for the religious order which lived in the monastery, no one, Indian, Mexican, or American, lived within fifty miles of the place. As far as anyone could tell, no one had ever lived there. The question was why had the monastery been built there in the first place? And why did the religious order continue to occupy it?

The last time Will and Gid were through there, Will had posed that same question to Father Francisco. With a small smile, Father Francisco had replied, "The answer is a mystery, and the mystery is the answer."

Will finally came to the conclusion that the monastery was there for no other purpose than to provide rest and water for the traveler. Anyone coming this way would have to stop at the monastery, for there was no other source of food or water within several miles in any direction.

He also realized that Kellett must know that, for, why else would his trail have led them there?

They reached the monastery just before dark. The abbey was surrounded by high stone walls and secured by a heavy oak gate. Gid pulled on a rope that was attached to a short section of log. The log swung away, then fell back, banging against the large, heavy gates with a booming thunder that resonated through the entire monastery. A moment later a small window slid open and a brown-hooded face appeared in the opening.

"Who are you?" the face asked.

For just a second, Will was confused. The face in the window belonged to Brother Miguel, and Will knew that Miguel knew them. Yet, Miguel was clearly acting as if he didn't.

"My name is Will Crockett. This is my brother, Gid."

"What do you want?"

"We are weary travelers. We want food, water, and shelter. Can't we come in?"

"I'm sorry. We can grant no entry."

"But, Brother, we are out of water. You cannot turn us away."

"I am truly sorry," the monk said. "God go with you." The little window slammed shut.

There was no way Miguel wouldn't have recognized them, so, from the moment Brother Miguel asked who they were, Will knew that something was wrong. That was why he didn't insist that they were known. Brother Miguel was trying to send them a message. The message had to be that Kellett and Alvarado were there.

Charley Kellett and Felix Alvarado had been standing just inside the gate when Will called. Alvarado was peering through the crack, between the timbers of the gate. "What are they doin' now?" Kellett asked.

"They ain't doin' nothin', 'cept just ridin' off," Alvarado answered.

Kellett chuckled, then put his pistol away. He looked at the short, overweight monk. "You done that real good, Padre," he said. "I don't think they suspect a thing."

"I am not a priest," Brother Miguel replied. "Therefore I am not addressed as Father."

"Yeah, well, brother, sister, father, padre, reverend, pastor, what the hell difference does it make? All you church guys are called somethin'. Come on, let's go see if the cook has our supper finished. I'm starvin'."

The three men walked back across the little courtyard, which, because of the irrigation and loving care bestowed upon it by the brothers of the order, was lush with flowers, fruit trees, and a vegetable garden. There were a dozen or more monks in the yard, each occupied by some specific task.

The building they entered was surprisingly cool, kept that way by the hanging ollas, which, while sacrificing some of the precious water by evaporation, paid off the investment by lowering the temperature by several degrees.

"Who was at the gate?" Father Francisco asked.

"Strangers, Father. I do not know who they were," Brother Miguel said. "They asked for food and water."

"And you denied them sanctuary?"

"I had no choice, Father," Brother Miguel said, rolling his eyes toward Kellett and Alvarado.

"You sent them away?" Father Francisco asked Kellett.

"We ain't exactly in the mood for visitors right now," Kellett answered.

"I see," Father Francisco said. "Still, to turn someone away is unthinkable. It is a show of Christian kindness to offer water, food, and shelter to those who ask it of us."

"You're showin' your Christian kindness by takin'

care of us," Kellett said. "Now, what about that food? How long does it take your cook to fix a little supper?"

"Forgive me for not mentioning it the moment you came in," Father Francisco said. "The cook has informed me that your supper is ready."

"Well, now, that's more like it! Why didn't you say somethin'?" Kellett growled. "Come on, Alvarado, let's get somethin' to eat."

"What is this?" Kellett asked, a moment later, when a bowl of beans and a plate of tortillas were set on the table before them.

"This is your supper."

"Is this it? Is this the Christian kindness you was talkin' about? You didn't even offer us no meat?" Kellett growled.

Father Francisco shook his head. "I'm sorry, in this order we do not eat meat. This is our regular fare. We cannot offer you what we do not have."

"I think maybe it is not so bad, Charley," Alvarado said, rolling up a tortilla in his fingers and filling it with the spicy beans.

"Yeah, well, you're a damn pepper-belly yourself so you like that shit," Kellett growled. "Me, now, I'm more of a meat and potatoes man."

Despite Kellett's protest, Alvarado showed no hesitation in eating.

Will and Gid waited about half an hour before they returned to the monastery. Leaving their horses hobbled, they slipped up to one of the side walls.

"What do we do now?" Gid asked.

"Now we climb over the wall," Will replied. Using chinks and holes in the stone facade to provide foot and handholds, Will started up the side of the wall.

"Damn, I was afraid that was what you were going to say," Gid said. He started up behind his brother, the task somewhat more laborious for him, because of his weight and size.

A moment later, both slipped over the top, then dropped to the ground on the inside.

Most of the buildings inside the monastery grounds were dark. Candles and oil for lamps were precious commodities to be used sparingly, though here and there a flickering light did manage to escape. It wasn't totally dark, however, for the moon was full and bright, and the chapel, dormitory, stable, storage, and grain buildings all gleamed in a soft, silver light, like white blooms sprouting from desert cactus.

"You go that way, I'll go this way," Will whispered. Gid nodded, and the two started on their mission.

The night was alive with the long, high-pitched trills and low viola-like thrums of the frogs. For counter melodies there were crickets and the long, mournful howl of coyotes. From the stable, a mule brayed and a horse whickered.

With his gun in hand, and staying in the shadows alongside the wall, Will moved toward the chapel. He found a window and looked inside. There, he saw two men with Father Francisco. The men were pointing their pistols at Father Francisco, who was holding a jewel-encrusted, silver chalice and gold cross clutched tightly to his chest.

"Please, Senor Kellett," he heard Father Francisco's pleading voice. "You cannot take the chalice and the cross. They are sacred relics, given to the service of God by the King of Spain more than two hundred years ago. Ten Abbots before me have kept them safe. I will not be the one who loses them."

"They're worth some money, ain't they?" Kellett asked.

"Yes."

"Then we're takin' 'em."

"You will have to kill me first," Father Francisco insisted.

Alvarado laughed, a high-pitched, rather insane chuckle. "You hear that, Charley? We'll have to kill him."

"Well hell, preacher man, that ain't goin' to be no problem," Kellett said. "Felix likes to kill, don't you, Felix?"

"Si, Senor," Alvarado said. He cocked his pistol, then pointed it at Father Francisco.

"Hold it!" Will shouted. Will was still outside the chapel, looking through the window, certainly not in the position he wanted to be to challenge them, but he had no choice. They were about to kill Father Francisco.

"What the hell! Who is that?" Alvarado shouted, swinging his gun toward the window. Kellett was standing by the only light in the room, a flickering candle. With danger imminent, he snuffed it out. The inside of the chapel was immediately plunged into darkness.

Will couldn't see anyone inside, but because he was outside, and lighted by the brightness of the moon, he was visible to both Kellett and Alvarado. They fired.

Will felt a hammer-blow to his shoulder. He returned fire, using the flame pattern from inside as his target. He heard someone groan, then fall. A moment later he heard a crash of glass from the other side of the building and he realized that someone had jumped through the window. He hurried around to try and head him off but, to his surprise, suddenly found himself growing very dizzy. After that, everything went black.

Gid was on the far corner of the grounds, sneaking up on the stable, when he heard the gunshots from the chapel. With his own gun in hand, he started running back through the dark, toward the sound of the shooting.

He heard a crash of glass, then he saw someone running through the shadows. He also saw Will in a splash of moonlight, and he saw him stagger, then fall.

"Will!" Gid shouted, starting toward his brother. He let the fleeing man run. For the moment, nothing was more important to him than the well-being of his brother.

Charley Kellett was the one who had leaped through the window and escaped into the night. Felix Alvarado was the man Will shot in the exchange of gunfire. Alvarado died before morning, and even though he was an outlaw who had bullied the Brothers of the Monastery and was in the process of stealing their most precious artifacts, the monks prayed over his body and buried him, if not in the consecrated graveyard, at least just outside the wall.

The bullet was taken from Will's shoulder, and he was patched up and tended by the Brothers of the order. Despite their nursing skills, however, Will contracted a fever and began drifting in and out of consciousness. For several hours, Gid didn't know if Will was going to pull through or not, and though he didn't participate in any of the formal prayers for recovery said by the Brothers, he did offer a few simple prayers of his own.

Unable to wait around and do nothing, Gid found things that would keep him busy. Early in the morning of the third day, he was repairing a door on the granary, when he saw Father Francisco coming toward him. He studied the priest's face, trying to determine if the news he bore was good or bad, but Father Francisco was so skilled in the art of stoicism, that it was impossible to tell.

"Brother Gideon," Father Francisco said. Nothing in the tone of his voice imparted any information.

"How is Will?" Gid asked, getting right to the point.

"God has smiled upon us," Father Francisco said. "Your brother will make a full recovery."

Gid smiled. "Thank you," he said.

"No, Brother Gideon. Thank God."

"Yeah," Gid said. "Yeah, I'm goin' to do that. Not the way you fellas do... but I promise you, I'm going to do that."

Over the next few days, while waiting for his brother to recover, Gid found much to admire in the way the monks lived their lives. Gid, who always had been much more a man of the soil than Will, particularly enjoyed working in the garden with them. And as he did so, he couldn't help but contrast his own life of danger and violence with the lives of quiet service and selfless devotion lived by the Brothers. He shared his thoughts with Father Francisco.

"The thing is, Father, I haven't always been a good man," Gid admitted. "I've drunk a lot, whored a lot, and I've killed. Though, mostly, I've only killed those who needed killing."

"It is not for us to judge who needs killing," Father Francisco said. "All are God's children. Do you think He loves some more and others less?"

"I don't know how God could possibly love some of the sons of bitches I've had to kill," Gid said.

"We can never understand the depth of God's love," Francisco said.

Chapter Five

Two Weeks Later

The terrible pain stopped and a warming numbness set in. It was the numbness that allowed Frank Wagner to keep up with the others on their mad ride away from the holdup. But with the numbness came also a weakness from loss of blood, and by the time they rode into the little town of Coneradero just before dawn the next morning, Wagner was staying in his saddle only by supreme will.

"Hey, Charley, Frank's about to keel over here," Donnie Hamilton said. Hamilton had taken it on himself to ride beside Wagner, and for the last three hours had held the reins to Wagner's horse, while Wagner used both hands on the pommel just to stay up.

"Stay with him," Charley ordered. Kansas Charley Kellett, never one to stay down long, had recovered from the loss of his partner Felix Alvarado by putting together a gang of outlaws and misfits. With them, he had hit the bank in Bonito, New Mexico.

It had been a very botched bank robbery. One of the tellers tried to run and they shot him, killing him, and a bank customer in the process. With the entire town alerted, there was nothing left to do but scoop up a handful of money from the open till. That netted them a grand total of two hundred and six dollars.

The alerted town reacted quickly, and even as they were mounting their horses, the good citizens of Bonito began shooting at them. Frank Wagner was hit as he climbed onto his horse, shot by a woman who was firing a rifle from just inside the door of the hardware store across the street.

"Maybe we can find a doctor in town to fix him up," Jasper Moody suggested.

"We don't have time," Charley growled. "That posse's goin' to be on us like stink on shit if we wait around here."

"He can't go on much longer, Charley. He needs a doctor," Hamilton insisted.

"He's gutshot ain't he? He's goin' to die anyway, ain't he? Takin' him to a doctor just to have him tell us Wagner is goin' to croak is just goin' to slow us down more."

"You're all heart, Charley," Wagner grunted.

"Yeah, well, we could just drop you off by the side of the road," Charley explained.

"That's a good idea. Why don't we do that?" Perry Hoyt asked.

"But look, we got to eat, ain't we?" Hamilton asked. "Maybe we could have the doc's woman fix us some hot grub while he's lookin' at Frank."

"We could do that, couldn't we, Charley? Donnie's right. We got to eat," Moody said.

"All right, all right," Charley agreed. "We'll stop, but just for long enough to get somethin' to eat."

It was still pre-dawn dark, but as the five men rode through the street, their way was lighted by squares of golden light on the ground, cast through the windows of the houses where early risers were already beginning to set to breakfast.

Charley halted them when they reached the end of the street.

"What is it?" Hamilton asked.

"You wanted to take him to the doc, didn't you? Well, that's the doc's house down there," Charley said.

"How do you know?"

"I was here once. You know, as I think back on it, the doc's got him a fine-lookin' woman, too. Don't know how an old fool like him got such a young, pretty wife. I seen 'er the first time, I thought she was his daughter."

The house Charley pointed to was a low, single-story building which set nearly half a block away from the others. A wisp of wood smoke rose from the chimney, carrying with it the aroma of frying bacon.

"Before we ride up there, fellas, take a good look around," Charley said. "Make sure nobody's watchin' us."

The saddles squeaked as the riders twisted to look around. Wagner held on, telling himself there was only a short time left, then he could lay down and rest in a nice, soft bed.

"It looks clear," Moody said.

"Let's go," Charley replied. He clicked to his horse and the five of them moved slowly across the distance. They stopped just in front of the doctor's house.

Clifton VanDyke, MD, the sign read by the door. Charley didn't bother to knock, he just pushed it open and barged in. Perry Hoyt and Donnie Hamilton were right behind him, half-carrying, half-supporting Wagner. Jasper Moody brought up the rear, looking around with his pistol drawn, making certain no one had seen them.

"What the—? What is this?" the surprised doctor asked, looking up from his breakfast table. His wife was standing at the stove frying bacon, and she looked around in alarm as well.

"Don't get fretted none, doc," Charley said. "I'm Charley Kellett. I reckon you've heard of me."

"Kansas Charley!" Dr. VanDyke gasped. "Yes, yes, of course I've heard of you."

Kellett's pictures decorated Wanted posters all over the Southwest, and as "Kansas Charley," he had been glamorized by being the subject of a half-dozen dime novels.

Charley grinned broadly. "Yeah, Kansas Charley, that's me," he said. He was proud of his notoriety, and, even though he couldn't read, he had a copy of each of the novels that had been written about him. "One of my men got hisself pretty bad shot up yesterday afternoon. He needs some doctorin'." Charley looked over toward the stove. "And the rest of us need some grub."

"What makes you think I would ..." Dr. VanDyke started, then he stopped and sighed. "Never mind, put him on the bed. Let me take a look at him."

Hamilton and Hoyt put Wagner on the bed. Dr. VanDyke sat beside him, then opened Wagner's shirt.

"He's lucky," he said. "I don't think there's any festering. But the bullet is going to have to come out."

"Hell, why bother?" Charley asked. "He's gutshot. That means he's goin' to die."

"Not necessarily. If I can get the bullet out and he doesn't start festering, he's got a chance."

"You want to waste your time on him, go right ahead. Me, I want somethin' to eat. Miss?"

"There's bacon and a skillet," the doctor's wife said. "And a basket of fresh eggs. There's also a pan of biscuits, fresh made. If you want breakfast, fix it yourself. I have to help my husband tend to this man's wound."

Charley pulled his pistol and pointed it at Wagner. "Well hell, if that's all that's getting' in the way of us getting' a little grub, I can just put him out of his misery now."

Dr. VanDyke stepped between Charley and Wagner. "If you shoot him, you're goin' to have to shoot me too," he said.

"All right by me," Charley said easily.

"And me," the woman added, stepping in front of her husband.

Charley looked at them for a moment longer, then chuckled. "All right, have it your way. Donnie, you fix the breakfast."

"Why me? I ain't no cook."

"I said fix the damn breakfast," Charley said, his voice flat and cold. "You the one wanted to get Frank tended to."

"All right, all right," Hamilton mumbled.

"Doc, you not only got yourself a young, pretty woman, you got a brave one, too," Charley said. "How did an old fart like you get someone like that?"

When Dr. VanDyke didn't answer, Charley gave them both an insolent smile and nod, then walked over to join the others at the kitchen stove.

"Here's a little laudanum," Dr. VanDyke said to

Wagner, handing him a small bottle. "Take it. You'll need it when I start probing for the bullet."

With his wife assisting, Dr. VanDyke removed Wagner's shirt, then began digging in the wound for the bullet. Charley, Hamilton, Moody, and Hoyt ate their breakfast, totally unconcerned with what was happening over on the bed. A few minutes later VanDyke announced that he had the bullet and dropped it with a clink into the pan of warm water. The bullet lay in the bottom of the pan with tiny bubbles of blood rising to paint a swirl of red on the water's surface. No one at the breakfast table seemed particularly interested in the medical report.

"You 'bout finished over there, Doc?" Charley asked, coming from the table, carrying a sandwich made from bacon and a biscuit.

"I've got the bullet out."

"Good, get him patched up so we can put him back on his horse."

"This man can't go anywhere," Dr. VanDyke said. "Why, if you take him out of here now, it'll kill him."

"He knew the chances, just like the rest of us," Charley said. "Frank," Charley said gruffly. "Come on, Frank. Get up!"

Wagner groaned.

"Why don't we leave him here, like the doc said?" Hamilton asked.

"We can't do that. He knows where we're goin'. He might talk."

"Wagner won't talk," Hamilton said. "He's a good man, he won't talk."

"We killed two people in that holdup," Charley said. "That means if we get caught, we're goin' to hang. If they tell him they won't hang him if he'll help 'em find us, are you tellin' me he won't talk?"

"Well, what are we goin' to do?" Hamilton asked. "I mean if we can't take him with us and we can't leave him here?"

Charley looked at Wagner, who was now unconscious. Then, without a word, and with as little thought as if he were stepping on a roach, he picked up a pillow and pushed it down over Wagner's face.

"What? What are you doing?" the doctor's wife gasped in shock. She reached for Charley, but he hit her in the face with a wicked backhand, which sent her careening backward, where she bounced off the wall, then slid down into a sitting position.

"Stop!" Dr. VanDyke said. "Stop, you're going to kill him!"

"Yeah, Doc, that's what I aim to do," Charley answered with a giggle.

Wagner began to struggle beneath the pillow and Charley pressed it down harder.

"Charley, look out!" Hoyt suddenly called, and Charley looked over to see Dr. VanDyke fumbling desperately with a shotgun, trying to close the breech.

Charley pulled his pistol and fired, his bullet hitting VanDyke right between the eyes. The doctor's wife screamed and Charley turned toward her.

"Shut up!" he shouted. "Shut up!"

She screamed again.

Charley fired a second time and the woman quit screaming. A tiny black hole appeared just over her left breast. A trickle of blood oozed down from the hole and her head slumped back against the wall, her eyes open and sightless.

"Shit!" Charley said. "I didn't want to do that. I'd planned to have a little fun with her first."

Outside and all through the neighborhood, dogs began to bark.

"What was that?" a distant voice called.

"Charley, we better get outta here!" Moody warned. "The whole town's done been woke up."

"What about Frank?" Hamilton asked.

Kellett took the pillow away from Wagner's face, then shot him between the eyes.

"What about him?" Kellett asked coldly.

Outside, they could hear dogs barking and people shouting.

"I think those shots come from the doc's house," they heard someone call.

"Let's get out of here," Kellett said.

At Charley's command, the four outlaws bolted through the front door, then vaulted up onto their horses. With the sun showing streaks of red in the eastern sky, they galloped out of town past a dozen or more townspeople, who were by then hurrying down to the doctor's house to see the carnage that had been left behind.

Three Nights Later

"You check the horses?" Moody asked as Hamilton came walking back into camp. "They could'a got loose in that storm last night. I wouldn't want to be out here on foot."

"They didn't go nowhere," Hamilton said. He sat down on a rock and picked up a stick to begin poking in the dirt. "Where do you think Charley is? You think he's somewhere spendin' our money? I wouldn't put it past the son of a bitch."

"You want to accuse him of that when he gets back?" Moody asked.

"If he gets back," Hamilton said with a growl.

"He'll be back," Moody said. "He's just out checkin' to see if anyone's on our trail. I figure that storm last night done us more good than about anythin'. It for

53

sure wiped out our tracks so's no one could trail us. A week or two with no trail to speak of and things are sure to calm down."

"How the hell you expect anything to die down? We killed two people in the bank holdup, then the doctor and his wife, to say nothin' of Frank Wagner."

Moody chuckled. "Hell, you don't think anyone got upset 'bout us killin' Wagner, do you?"

"Maybe not... but we done enough other stuff to have the whole world lookin' for us," Hamilton suggested.

"Yeah, well, if you hadn't insisted we get Frank a doctor, we wouldn't a had to kill the doctor and his wife," Moody accused.

"Wagner was hurtin' somethin' awful," Hamilton said. "You wouldn't let a horse suffer like he was."

"You'd shoot a horse," Hoyt suggested.

"Yeah, well Charley offered to shoot the son of a bitch," Moody suggested. "But you wouldn't have none of it. Now, look where we are, scurryin' around out here like hunted animals, with practically no money a'tall." He leaned over the fire and looked at the meat he was roasting. "This here rabbit looks about done."

"This is a hell of a breakfast, ain't it? I'm getting' damned tired of rabbit and squirrel and prairie chicken and the like," Hamilton growled. "I want a steak."

"And people in hell want ice water," Hoyt said.

"Shut up your bitchin'. You don't want any rabbit, fine. Me an' Moody will eat your part."

"Didn't say I wasn't goin' to eat it. Just said I was tired of it."

Hamilton took out his knife and started to cut off a piece of rabbit. Just as he did so, however, there was a loud popping sound, then the smack of a bullet crashing into the rabbit. Pieces of the rabbit flew in every direction.

Hamilton let out a shout of fear and alarm and jumped back from the rabbit. The other two men jumped up and pulled their guns.

"Just drop 'em right there," a voice called.

"What the hell? Who are you, mister? Show yourself!" Hoyt shouted.

There was another gunshot, and this time the bullet hit the ground right between Hoyt's feet, then ricocheted up between his legs and whined out over the open prairie.

"I'll take off your balls with the next shot," the voice growled.

"No, no!" Hoyt said, dropping his gun and raising his hands. "We give up! We give up!"

Moody and Hamilton dropped their guns and raised their hands as well.

"That's more like it," the disembodied voice said. There was the sound of boots walking on rocky ground, then two men appeared from behind a rock. One of them was carrying handcuffs, and he tossed them forward. "How about you fellas trying these on for size?" he asked. He looked around the camp. "Where's Kellett?"

"The son of a bitch skedaddled on us," Hamilton said. "With our money." Hamilton squinted as he stared at the two men. "Who the hell are you? You ain't the law."

"I reckon not. I'm Will Crockett. This here is my brother, Gid. You boys stirred up quite a ruckus when you robbed that bank in Bonito. You're worth five-hundred dollars apiece."

"Will and Gid Crockett? I've heard of you," Hoyt said.

"A lot of people have" Will said.

"Since when did you boys become bounty hunters? Way I've heard it, you walk on the wrong side of the law more often than not."

"Bounty hunting isn't something we're goin' to do, permanent," Will said. "Just long enough to see Charley Kellett dead."

"Well, hell, what's that got to do with us? You can see, he ain't here."

"Maybe not, but you boys had the bad luck to be with him," Will said. "We were looking for him and we just naturally found you. And, like I said, you're worth five-hundred dollars apiece. When we see money like that, we have to pick it up. Get 'em mounted, Gid."

Gid took his rope and made three nooses. He put the nooses around the necks of each of his prisoners, before ordering them to mount up. As Hamilton started to get on his horse, he slipped, causing a pull against the neck of the other two men.

"Careful there, you dumb bastard!" Moody growled. "You want to break all our necks?"

Once all three prisoners were mounted, Gid tied the end of the rope to his saddle, then swung up onto his horse.

"Okay, gents," he said easily. "Let's head for Bonito. And I would suggest that you all stay together. If one of you tries to run ... you're just likely to break the necks of all three."

Chapter Six

Will Crockett watched the dust rise from the hoof falls of his three prisoners, and he thought about the fact that Charley Kellett was still a free man. Moody had taunted them about it, obviously trying to get a rise out of Will or Gid. What Moody didn't realize was that he came much closer than he expected, because the subject of Charles Kellett was even more sensitive now than it had been when he and Gid had started their quests.

There was seldom a day that went by that he didn't think about Kellett, and whenever he rode into a new town, he found that he was always looking for a big man with yellow eyes, a drooping eyelid, and a puffed, ugly scar.

Will looked over at his brother, and wondered if Gid was as tired as he was. It wasn't just the ass-sore tiredness of a long, hard ride. It was the kind of bone-deep weariness that comes on a man after years of riding the trail with one dusty town behind his back and another just ahead. The bad side of it was that it would never get any better. The good side was that, at this stage, it could get no worse.

This anchorless drifting had become a part of the Crockett brothers' heritage. They were men redefined by the saloons, cow towns, stables, manure-piled streets, and open prairies they had encountered. They could not deny this without denying their own existence, and, in fact, had no intention of ever doing so. They were a long way from home, both in time and distance, and yet they were as close to home as the nearest hotel, back room of a saloon, or whore's bed.

"Hey, Crockett, you two goin' to push us all night, or are we goin' to get a chance to rest a bit?" Moody asked.

"Just keep movin'," Will growled. "We'll be there by midnight."

"Midnight?" Moody complained. "What the hell? You jumped us 'fore daylight this mornin'. You got no right to push us 'till midnight. I've heard tell that peace officers have to give their prisoners proper rest, food, an' water."

Gid laughed. "Well there you go, mister. Neither one of us is a peace officer," he said. "Besides, I wouldn't be worryin' a whole lot about rest if I was you. You and your friends will be getting an eternity of rest in just about a week or so."

"Yeah? Well, we'll see about that," Moody replied.

"Moody, you said if we teamed up with Charley Kellett they'd never catch us." Hoyt whimpered. "I don't want to hang, Moody. You hear me? I don't want to hang."

"Shut up, Perry," Moody said. "Ain't nothin' to be gained by whimperin'."

"All of you keep quiet," Gid said. "I'm not in any mood to listen to your prattle."

"How 'bout if I sing a little song?" Hamilton started. "Buffalo Gals won't you come out tonight, come out tonight, come out—uhnn!"

The sudden end to his song was brought on by Gid jerking hard on the rope. As the rope was looped around Hamilton's neck, it had the effect of choking off his efforts.

"Watch it!" Hamilton said. "If you ain't careful, you could jerk me off here an' break my neck!"

"Really? Well, now, I wouldn't want to do that now, would I, Donnie?" Gid said. "That would spoil everyone's fun in watching you hang."

"I hate disappointin' all those nice folks like that, Crockett," Moody said with a growl. "But I ain't plannin' on givin' them a show."

Despite the protests, Will and Gid pushed their three prisoners far into the night, arriving in Bonito so late that three of the four saloons were already dark, and the fourth, though still showing light from the bottom floor, was quiet. The horses plodded down the dirt street, the hollow clopping echoing back from the darkened false-fronted stores and houses. From the back of one of the houses a baby cried, and Will heard the cooing sound of its mother going to comfort it. Such sounds barely penetrated Will's cognizance. He was aware that another world existed outside the world he and his brother occupied. He knew there was an entire world of husbands and wives, children and homes, schools, churches, and socials, but such things were so remote from his own experience that he was unable to even dredge up a twinge of envy or regret for his exclusion.

The jail, like the other buildings in town, was dark. They stopped in front, and Will swung down from his horse.

"Ha!" Moody barked in what might have been a laugh. "The sheriff an' his deputies have all gone home for the night. You're goin' to have to bring us back tomorrow."

"You could take us over to the hotel, maybe rent us a room," Hamilton suggested.

"Hotel, hell! How 'bout takin' us down to the saloon? We could prob'ly find some whores that'll share their bed with us tonight," Moody said.

"Don't know 'bout these two boys, though," Hamilton added. "What self-respectin' whore would have anythin' to do with either one of them?"

Will tied his horse off at the hitch rail, then stepped

up onto the wooden porch in front of the jail. His boots clumped loudly across the boards. When his horse whickered, he spun around quickly, pistol in hand, the hammer pulled back. Just as he had suspected, the three were trying to ease out of the hitch. Gid gave a jerk and all three of them felt it in their necks.

"Hold it, hold it!" Moody said. "We ain't planning on goin' nowhere!"

"Moody, that's just about the first true words you've spoken," Gid said. "You're not goin' anywhere." He emphasized his comment with another jerk on the rope, hard enough to make all three men grunt in protest.

Seeing that his brother had things well in control, Will turned around and banged loudly on the front door of the jail house.

"What do you want?" a muffled voice called from inside.

"Open the door. I've got some prisoners for you."

"Prisoners? We wasn't expectin' no prisoners. Who might they be?"

"Jasper Moody, Perry Hoyt, Donnie Hamilton," Will answered.

"What the hell? You got 'em?" the voice called. Will could hear footsteps from inside. A key rattled in the lock, and a moment later the door opened. A man, obviously rousted from sleep, stood there, wearing boots and a pair of long underwear. "Who are you?" he asked.

"I'm Will Crockett." Will nodded toward Gid. "The handsome fella hanging onto the rope is my brother, Gid."

"Crockett? Wait a minute. Durin' the war, wasn't you two boys part of the Bushwhackers?"

"You going to take these prisoners or not?"

"Yes, yes sir, I'll take 'em," the man said. "I'm Deputy Isaac Green, Mr. Crockett. Boy, oh boy, is Sheriff McIvor goin' to be surprised, come mornin'."

The deputy reached up beside the door. When he pulled his hand back, it was clutched around a Greener ten-gauge shotgun. He pointed the double-barreled weapon at the three men.

"Okay, you boys, just climb on down real easy now," he said. "I've got a nice room all ready for you."

"These men are worth five-hundred dollars each," Will said. "I'll be needing you to sign a receipt."

"I ain't got no money to give you two boys, Mr. Crockett. I'm just the deputy 'round here."

"That's all right," Will said. "All you have to do is sign the receipt, tellin' that we brought them in. We'll take care of the rest."

"Sure thing. I'll be proud to do that soon as I get these critters locked up. Come along, boys." He jabbed one of them with a shotgun.

"Hey, watch it. That hurts," Moody complained.

"Does it?" the deputy asked, jabbing him again. "Well, now, that's too bad."

Fifteen minutes later Will and Gid were standing at the bar over in the First Rate Saloon.

"Got any Old Overholt?" Will asked when the bartender moved down to stand in front of him.

The bartender, who was sucking on a toothpick, nodded without speaking, then turned to pull a bottle down from the wall behind him. He poured a glass and slid it down the bar in front of Will.

"You the fellas that brung in them three killers and robbers a while ago?" the bartender asked.

Will nodded, then tossed the drink down.

"Seen you comin' in," the bartender said. "Me 'n Tillie 'n Blanch was the onliest ones down here, an' we heard the horses, so we looked out to see who it was."

"Who was they?" one of the two women asked. The lantern light was kind to both of them from where Will stood. Their skin glowed soft and golden, and the dissipation of the life they led didn't show so badly. They both managed to look almost as young as their years.

"Jasper Moody, Perry Hoyt, and Donnie Hamilton," Will answered.

"Kellett wasn't with them?" the bartender asked.

"No."

"That's a shame. He's the worst of the bunch. I'd

really like to see him brought in."

"We'll get him," Gid said.

"Lots of folks have said that," the bartender replied. "He ain't been got yet."

"We'll get him," Gid said again.

"Well, if you ask me, I'm glad you got some of 'em," Tillie said. She walked down to stand beside Will, and Blanch, taking her tip from Tillie, walked down to stand next to Gid. "Cy, pour these two fellas another drink, on us," Tillie said.

"Thanks," Will replied, as Cy refilled the glasses.

"It was bad enough them killin' that teller and poor Mr. Mondell when they robbed the bank here," Blanch said. "But I heard what they done over in Coneradero to that poor Dr. VanDyke and his wife. And the VanDykes doin' no more than their Christian duty to succor the wounded. Whenever Kellett finally is caught, his will be one hangin' that I don't aim to miss."

The light was less kind to the two women up close, but there was still something appealing about them. Maybe it was the good humor in their eyes, still alive despite the brutality of their profession. Maybe it was the swell of breasts, soft and inviting to someone many weeks on the trail. Or maybe the two boys were just bone-tired and needed someone to help them make it through the rest of the night.

Chapter Seven

"All Rise!"

There was a scrape of chairs, a rustle of pants, petticoats, and skirts as the spectators in the courtroom stood. A spittoon rang as one male member of the gallery made a last-second, accurate expectoration of his tobacco quid.

"Oyez, oyez, oyez. This court is now in session. The Honorable Ernest Fowler presiding."

The gallery was limited to fifty spectators, and tickets for attendance were highly prized commodities. Most people agreed that Judge Fowler's performances were the best show anywhere, not because of any particular showmanship, but because of his hard-nosed treatment of criminals. He had sentenced so many hardened criminals to hang that he was known far and wide as "King of the Gallows."

Judge Fowler stepped through a rear door and

viewed his court. He wasn't a tall man, but he was robust, with a square face and piercing blue eyes. He moved quickly to the bench, then sat down.

"Be seated," he said.

The gallery sat, then watched with interest as first the prisoners were brought into the room, and then the jury.

The jury, composed of twelve men, good and true, had listened to testimony from witnesses to the bank robbery and from the citizens of Coneradero. The witnesses from Coneradero told of hearing shots and seeing Charley Kellett, Jasper Moody, Donnie Hamilton, and Perry Hoyt ride away from the doctor's house. These same witnesses also testified that they found the doctor and his wife dead, along with a fifth member of their gang, Frank Wagner.

Now the jury was ready to render their verdict.

"Gentlemen of the jury, have you reached a verdict?" Judge Fowler asked.

"We have, Your Honor," the foreman answered.

"Please publish the verdict."

"We find the defendants, Jasper Moody, Donnie Hamilton, and Perry Hoyt, guilty of murder in the first degree, Your Honor."

"By God, you won't be hanging me!" Moody shouted.

"Bailiff, silence that prisoner," Judge Fowler said.

The bailiff glared at Moody.

ROBERT VAUGHAN

"Bailiff, would you position the prisoners before the bench for sentencing, please?" Judge Fowler asked.

"Yes, Your Honor."

The three men were brought before the bench, where they stood with their heads bowed, contritely.

The judge picked up his gavel and banged it once.

"I sentence you three men, Perry Hoyt, Donnie Hamilton, and Jasper Moody, to be hanged by the neck until you be dead. Sentence will be carried out at two o'clock on this very afternoon."

There was a buzz of whispering excitement throughout the court as everyone realized that on that very day there would be a multiple hanging of three prisoners.

"Three! Three at one time, by God!" someone said excitedly.

"Silence! Silence in the court," Judge Fowler said, and again, he slapped his gavel against the pad. The gallery grew quiet. "Deputy, escort the condemned men to the holding cells. Court is dismissed."

"Who'll have tickets to the hanging?" the clerk called.

"Me! I want one!" someone called.

"Save one for me!"

The three prisoners, their legs hobbled with an eighteen-inch chain were chained together for the move back to the cells. As the deputy escorted them out of the court and to the holding cell, they moved with an awkward gait. They shuffled out as crowds of people pressed around the clerk to get the little blue ticket which would grant them access to the side courtyard where the hanging would take place.

The holding cell was separate from the main jail. It was out in the side courtyard, less than fifty feet from the gallows itself. There, the condemned prisoners would be able to look through the barred windows and watch the crowd gather and the excitement grow as time for their execution approached.

The deputy took them out through the side door of the courthouse, then across the sun-baked, dirt-packed courtyard toward the little holding cell. It was quiet in the yard, since, as yet, no spectators had been allowed around the gallows.

As they passed through the shadow of the gallows, they saw someone up on the gallows deck, oiling the hinges to the trap door. He pulled the lever and the door swung open with a bang. Hamilton let out a little cry of alarm. The bailiff laughed.

"Don't you fret none, Donnie boy," the deputy teased. "They're just greasin' the doors to hell for you." He laughed out loud at his own joke.

"You're getting' a big kick out of this, ain't you, Isaac?" Moody said to the deputy.

"Oh, yeah," the deputy answered, smiling broadly.

"Watchin' you three boys hang is goin' to be like Christmas, New Years, and my birthday all rolled into one," he said.

"Isaac, I sure hope nothin' happens to upset your little plans," Moody said.

The deputy laughed out loud. "Still makin' the jokes, I see, eh, Jasper? Well, you may as well enjoy what time you got left. I sure plan to."

"I'm glad I can be so entertainin'," Moody said. He pointed toward the outhouse. "Hey Isaac, before you put us in our cells, how about lettin' me take a leak?"

"You just wait a while," the deputy answered.

"Accordin' to what the judge just said, I don't have all that long to wait for anything," Moody replied. "Besides, you want me to pee in my pants? Now, that would be a pretty sight for the ladies that come to see the hangin', won't it?"

The deputy looked around the courtyard. Except for the worker on the gallows, no one else was in sight.

"All right," he finally relented. "I'll let you take a leak. But be quick about it."

"Thanks," Moody said. "You are goin' to cut me loose from the others, aren't you? I don't care to have them all goin' in there with me."

The deputy laughed. "Why, Moody, I never knew you were such a shy man," he said. He bent down to un-lock the chain. He didn't notice that the man who had been working on the gallows had come down and was walking over toward him. As soon as he was even with the deputy, he pulled a gun and pointed it at Isaac's head.

"Unlock the hobble-chain too," the gallows worker said. "And get the others."

The deputy looked up in surprise, then his face reflected his shock.

"Kellett!" he gasped.

"Charley, you come for us!" Hamilton said.

"Sure, I come for you. You boys didn't think I was goin' to let my pards hang, did you?"

"I have to admit, I had my doubts," Hoyt said happily.

"Me, too," Hamilton added.

There were four horses tied up behind the courthouse.

"We'd best hurry," Kellett urged. "I had to knife the guard at the back gate."

Suddenly two guards came into the courtyard from the front of the building.

"Stop!" one of them shouted. He fired a shot, which missed. Kellett returned fire and he didn't miss. The guard who had fired collapsed with a hole in his chest. The other guard, suddenly realizing that he was alone, retreated back around the corner.

"We've got to get out of here!" Hamilton shouted.

"Wait a minute," Moody said. "I got a little busi-

ROBERT VAUGHAN

ness to take care of first." He looked at the deputy and
started smiling.

The deputy, realizing what was on Moody's mind,
began to tremble in fear, and he held his hands out in
front of him.

"Now, Jasper, you don't want to shoot me," he said.
"What good will that do you?"

"Oh, it'll do me a world of good, Isaac. More good
than you'll ever know," Moody said with a broad, evil
smile. He picked up the guard's gun and fired. A bullet hole
appeared in the deputy's forehead, then he pitched back.

"Come on, boys, let's ride!" Kellett shouted, swinging into his saddle.

By now the shouts and gunfire had alerted the others, and several armed men appeared in the courtyard,
just in time to see the four riders gallop through the
back gate. They fired at the outlaws, but not one bullet
found its mark. Kansas Charley Kellett and the entire
band had gotten away.

Chapter Eight

That Same Afternoon

Nearly three-hundred people, who had not yet heard of the mass escape, came to see the three men hanged. When they learned that the condemned prisoners had escaped, they were openly vocal in their disappointment at being cheated out of such a grand spectacle.

There was one condemned prisoner, a man named Darnell, who had raped and murdered a school marm. He wasn't due to die for one more week, but because the gallows had already been built and because Judge Fowler didn't want to disappoint the people, he moved the hanging up. With the others gone, Darnell was the only show in town.

"At least we're goin' to see a hangin' of some kind," the citizens told each other. "I mean, it ain't like comin' into town was a total waste."

On the second floor of the courtroom, Judge Fowler stood at the window of his chambers, looking down on the milling crowd. Will and Gid were just behind him. Gid lit a cigar, which he had just extracted from a humidor on the Judge's desk.

"I told you I'd pay the money and I will," Judge Fowler said without turning around. "There's fifteen hundred dollars in that brown envelope on my desk."

Will reached for it.

"The territory will pay another fifteen hundred to get them back, and I'll see to it that the court adds fifteen hundred more. That's a total of forty-five hundred dollars," Fowler said.

"Forty-five hundred dollars?" Will said. "You know, Judge, with that kind of reward money out there, you're just going to make it harder to find them. There will be too many people who don't know what they are doing, trying to get the reward. They'll just be getting in the way."

Judge Fowler turned away from the window. "That reward isn't for everyone," he said. "I'm only offering that to you."

"You're not putting out new dodgers?"

Judge Fowler shook his head. "No," he said.

"Why not? That kind of money is pretty persuasive," Gid replied.

"Like you say, it would just bring in too many amateurs. I particularly want these men," Judge Fowler said. "The reward is for dead or alive," Judge Fowler said. "But if you can, I want them alive. I want to hang these men."

"Where Kellett is concerned, we make no promises," Will said.

"You'll at least try to get them here alive?"

"Like I said, where Kellett is concerned, we make no promises," Will said again.

Judge Fowler stroked his chin for a long moment before he answered.

"All right," he said. "I've sentenced them to die, I guess the manner of their execution doesn't really matter. You do whatever it takes."

Billy Darnell looked around defiantly as he was led to the gallows. He was wearing a gray, collarless shirt and gray trousers. His legs weren't hobbled, but his hands were cuffed behind his back. He squirted out a stream of tobacco juice just as he reached the foot of the thirteen steps, then he hesitated.

"This ain't fair," Darnell said. "I wasn't supposed to hang 'til next week."

"Get on up there, Darnell," Sheriff McIvor said. "You done your killin' like a man, now die like one."

Darnell turned around to glare at him. "Sheriff, you don't have to give me no lessons on how to die," he said.

"Come on, Billy," McIvor said more gently. "The sooner we get this over with, the better it is for all of us."

Darnell moved onto the scaffold, then was positioned under the noose. The scaffold had been built for a multiple hanging, and it looked somewhat unbalanced with him standing at one end. From here, Darnell had a very good look into the faces of the spectators, and he glared at them defiantly.

The clergyman who was on hand for the hanging walked up to Darnell.

"Mr. Darnell, do you want to repent?" the clergyman asked.

"What have I got to repent for?"

"Why, you have killed, sir."

Darnell looked out over the faces of the crowd. "Yeah? Well, what do you think they are about to do to me?"

"The authorities are merely executing their God-given right," the preacher said.

"And the folks here? Is it their God-given right to enjoy watchin' me dance?"

"I beg of you, Sir. Repent. Repent now, before it is too late."

"I ain't repentin' for a goddamned thing."

"Mr. Darnell!" the preacher said angrily. "You are goin' to meet God with heresy in your heart and blasphemy on your lips! You'll spend an eternity in hell for that!"

"Thanks for the words, preacher," Darnell said sarcastically. "They're real comfortin'."

The preacher, red-faced with anger, turned and walked quickly off the scaffold.

"Any last words, Darnell?" the sheriff asked. The sheriff was having to serve as the hangman, since Kellett had killed the man who was supposed to do the job.

"Yeah. I wonder what they'll be servin' for supper in hell?" Darnell asked. "Whatever it is, it's bound to be better'n that pig swill you serve in this jail."

"I don't know, but when you get there, say hello to a few of my friends for me, will you?" the sheriff asked.

"Sheriff, you want me to hold you a place at the supper table?" Darnell asked as the black hood was slipped over his head.

The sheriff chuckled. "That's nice of you, Billy. Real nice," he said. "It's time." He fit the noose. "When the trap opens, don't hunch up your shoulders," he added, trying to be helpful. "Just relax and it'll be better."

"Really? How the hell do you know?" Darnell mumbled from under his hood.

When the sheriff had him ready, he stepped over to the handle that would open the trap door. He glanced

up toward the window where Judge Fowler stood looking down. Fowler nodded his head and the hangman
pulled the handle.

The trap door swung down on its hinges and Darnell's body dropped about five feet. There was an almost
orgasmic gasp from the crowd as the body fell.

Darnell didn't die right away. He was still alive,
and for almost four minutes he kept drawing his body
up as if in that way he could relieve the weight on his
neck. His stomach heaved, and those nearest the scaffold could hear rasping sounds from his throat. Finally
his body was still.

"Ghastly business this," Judge Fowler said, pour-
ing himself a drink with shaking hands. He looked over
at Will and Gid. "You two men live your lives right on
the edge, don't you?"

"You might say that," Will agreed.

Judge Fowler tossed his drink down. "Watch your
step," he said. "I wouldn't want to ever see either one or
both of you up there on my gallows."

"Don't worry, Judge," Will replied matter-of-factly.
"If it ever came to that... you wouldn't live long enough
to see it."

Nervously, Judge Fowler poured himself another
drink.

The sound of a shot rolled down the mountainside, picked up resonance, then echoed back from the neighboring mountains. Charley Kellett, who was holding a smoking pistol, turned toward his audience of three with a smile on his face. He had just broken a discarded whiskey bottle with his marksmanship.

"I'd like to see either one of the Crockett boys do that," he snarled.

"Charley, there ain't nobody said you ain't good with a gun," Hamilton said. "Maybe even as good as the Crocketts, but..."

"Maybe as good? Maybe as good?"

"Well, as good then. Maybe even better—"

"There ain't no maybe to it. I am better."

"But even if you are, that don't matter. You should'a seen how them sneaky bastards come up on us the last time. They got the drop on us afore we even had a notion anyone was anywhere around. I say we don't take no chances this time."

"And what do you propose that we do?" Charley asked.

"I think we ought to split up... ever' man for hisself. Them sons of bitches can't follow us all at the same time."

"No, but they can follow just one of us," Hoyt pointed out. "And woe betide the one that they follow."

"Yeah? Well, I ain't afraid of either one of the

bastards," Kellett said.

"You mean you don't care if they get on your tail?" Hamilton asked.

"Hell, when you get right down to it, they been on my tail ever' since the end of the war," Kellett replied. "What I ought to do is quit runnin'. I ought to just wait behind a rock and shoot 'em down."

"You mean you'd shoot 'em from ambush?" Hamilton asked.

"Hell yes! I don't need to kill the sons of bitches fair and square ... I just want to kill 'em."

"Charley has a point," Hoyt said. "The best way to handle the Crocketts would be to set up an ambush."

"No," Hamilton replied. "I still think it would be best if they didn't even find us at all, and if we split up, we'll have a better chance."

"Except for the one they come after," Hoyt pointed out.

"All right," Moody said. "How about this? Instead of all of us separatin', we'll break into two groups. That way they'll still have to make a choice, but even when they do, we won't have to face 'em alone."

"All right, I'll go along with that," Hoyt said.

"This is the way we'll do it," Charley explained. "Perry, you and Donnie cut out one way, me an' Moody will go another. Now, whichever ones of us gets wind that they ain't on our trail, why, we'll double back and help out the others. That way, we'll have 'em pinched right in the middle."

"Why that's a wonderful idea!" Hamilton said, smiling broadly. He chuckled. "Charley, you should'a been a general."

Chapter Nine

It was four days before Will and Gid came across a fresh trail. The men they were after had split up, two going in one direction, two going in the other. Will and Gid decided not to split up, but to follow one set of tracks.

"They'll probably rejoin somewhere," Will said. "And if they don't, why we'll take care of these two, then go after the others."

"Yeah," Gid agreed. "I just hope Kellett is one of the two men we're following."

Kellett wasn't one of the two. They learned that when they talked to a bartender in Aleman. He had recognized Donnie Hamilton when he stopped for a drink.

Hamilton was with another man ... the bartender wasn't sure who the other man was, but he was sure it wasn't Kansas Charley Kellett.

It was too late now to double back and follow the

other trail. They had no choice but to stay on this one and hope that their theory of them eventually rejoining was right.

Hamilton and whoever was with him took great pains to cover their true trail, while leaving false trails for the Crocketts to follow. They rode through streams and over hard rock, trying every trick in the book to shake off their pursuers but, doggedly, Will and Gid hung on.

Once, while following them through a draw in Salt Rock Mesa, Hamilton and his partner started a rock slide. It nearly caught Will and Gid, and they had to turn their horses and gallop hard to get out of the way.

"Damn!" Hoyt said. "We almost got the sons of bitches!"

"Yeah, well, almost ain't good enough," Hamilton said. "The bastards are still alive, and they're still after us."

"What are we goin' to do, Donnie? You got 'ny ideas?"

"No," Hamilton answered.

"What if we just wait behind some rocks somewhere and ambush them?"

Hamilton shook his head. "If we don't get 'em right off, they'll get behind us and then we'll be in a gunfight with 'em. I don't know about you, Perry, but I ain't plannin' on getting' in no gunfight with the likes of Will and Gid Crockett. Not with it bein' just the two of us."

"Yeah, well it ain't supposed to be just the two of

us," Hoyt reminded him. "Charley said him and Moody would come a runnin' if they seen that the Crocketts wasn't after them. Remember?"

"Yeah? Well where the hell are they?" Hamilton asked. "Do you see any sign of 'em?"

"No," Hoyt admitted.

"No, an' you ain't likely to," Hamilton told him. "Them two sons of bitches have run out on us."

Twenty Miles South

"Did you see anything back there, Moody?" Kellett asked when Moody scrambled back down from the promontory, his boots dislodging pebbles and small rocks.

"No, nothin'," Moody replied. He brushed his hands together. "I looked as far as I could in all directions, and I didn't see even a piece of a dust plume. I don't think they're followin' us."

Kellett took a drink of water, wiped the back of his hand across his mouth, then corked his canteen and hooked it back on the saddle pommel.

"Well, then they must've lit out after Hamilton and Hoyt."

"We goin' to double back?" Moody asked.

"Double back? What for?"

"You said we was goin' to double back if we seen that the Crocketts wasn't doggin' us."

"Far's I'm concerned, Hamilton and Hoyt is on their own. Unless you want to go back and tangle with the Crockett boys."

"You think I'm crazy? If you ain't goin' back, I sure as hell ain't."

"I didn't figure you was that dumb," Charley said. "Anyway, the way I look at it, by the Crocketts takin' out after them like they done, just makes it all the better for us."

"Yeah," Moody said. He smiled. "Yeah, I guess you're right at that. While Hamilton and Hoyt is keeping the Crocketts busy, we'll be runnin'. The question is, where will we be runnin' to?"

"You ever heard of the town of Dona Ana?"

"No, can't say as I have."

"Well, it's a little fly speck of a town not too far from here," Kellett said. "There's a man there, name of Ralph Hopkins. He's a good man with a gun, and an old pard of mine. When I left the bunch of you before, I sent Hopkins a wire, askin' him to join up with us. If the Crocketts run into us, it might come in handy to have an extra gun."

"We had two extra guns, and you sent 'em off," Moody said.

"Yeah, but it worked out fine, what with the Crocketts goin' after them. Besides, both them together ain't as good a gun as Hopkins."

"What makes you think Hopkins would join us? Who would just volunteer to start runnin' from the Crocketts?"

"Hopkins is good with a gun, but he ain't too swift up here," Kellett said, tapping the side of his head. "He needs someone to figure things out for him. I figure we'll join up in Dona Ana, then move over to a little town not too far from here, called Crawford. We'll rob the bank there. Then we'll not only have an extra gun ridin' with us ... we'll have some money to spend."

"Crawford? Never heard of that one either. How big is it?"

"No more'n two or three-hundred people."

"No more'n two or three-hundred? How much money could be in a bank like that?" Moody asked.

"Well, how much you got now?" Kellett asked.

"Not much," Moody admitted.

"So whatever we get ought to sound pretty good, don't you think?" Kellett asked. "Besides, I'm talkin' about a real cracker box of a bank. Prob'ly ain't nobody ever even thought about robbin' it. Hell, the folks will be so surprised, they'll piss in their pants when they see us."

Twenty Miles North

"They're still comin'," Hoyt said.

Hamilton twisted around in his saddle. "How far

back are they? Can you see 'em?"

"Yeah, I got a glimpse of 'em just over the last ridge."

"That'd make 'em less'n a mile back."

"Ain't they no way we can shake 'em?" Hoyt asked.

"You got 'ny ideas that we ain't tried?" Hamilton replied. "We done ever'thing I can think of, an' it ain't even slowed 'em down none."

"So what do you want to do now? You want to wait behind a couple of rocks like I suggested?"

"No. I told you, I don't want to get into a gunfight with 'em unless the odds are a little better."

"Well, pretty soon we ain't gonna have no choice," Hoyt pointed out. "They're back there, they're comin', and they ain't nothin' on earth goin' to stop 'em from catchin' us. Then we're goin' to have to shoot it out sure enough, only by then they'll be choosing the time and the place."

"Yeah, well there is one thing we could do," Hamilton suggested, "if you're game for it."

"Hell, I'm willin' to try 'bout anythin'," Hoyt said. "What you got in mind?"

"We could split up again. You go one way and I'll go the other."

"Well now, hold it. That don't make no sense to me at all. I mean here you are, bitchin' 'cause you say two on two ain't the right kind of odds to go up against 'em. But you're wantin' us to split up so it'll be one to one."

"They didn't separate when we split up before. Like as not, they won't split up again. That means curtains for whoever's trail they dog," Hamilton said. "But the other one of us can get away free and clear. That gives each one of us a fifty-fifty chance of not havin' to run into 'em at all. And for whichever one of us that does run into him, well, hell, we won't be that much worse off than we are now."

"Yeah, all right," Hoyt said, stroking his chin. "I guess them odds is about as good as any. Which way you aimin' to go?"

"I thought I might go west," Hamilton said.

"All right, you go west, I'll go south," Hoyt replied. He smiled crookedly at Hamilton. "I ain't goin' to wish you luck," he said. " 'Cause if your luck is runnin' good, that'll mean mine is runnin' bad."

"Yeah," Hamilton said. "I know what you mean. Maybe we'll see each other around some time."

"Maybe," Hoyt replied. He slapped his heels against his horse's flanks, then started down the middle of a small stream, heading south.

Hamilton started west, but after a few moments he reined up and looked back to the point where he and Hoyt had separated. Hoyt was out of sight now, and, because he had gone down the middle of the stream, there was absolutely no sign that he had been there at all.

Hamilton saw a willow tree, its boughs hanging low

over the water, and he suddenly got an idea. He rode back into the stream, up to the tree, then he reached up and broke two of the branches. After that he rode back into the rocks, got off his horse and tied it down. He pulled the Winchester from its saddle sheath and bellied down between two rocks, where he not only had cover and concealment, but a good view of the willow tree as well. He jacked a round into the chamber, then piled a couple of rocks on top of each other to make a rest for the rifle. He sighted down the barrel, then waited.

When Will and Gid reached the edge of the stream, they stopped. If the two men they were after followed the pattern they had established, they would use the stream for as long as they could, to avoid leaving a trail. For most trackers that would work. Will and Gid, however, could often follow a trail through the water by paying attention to such things as rocks dislodged against the flow of water or silt, which, when disturbed by horse's hooves would leave a little pattern in the water for several minutes afterward.

Gid was about to check the streambed when he saw something unusual. There were two limbs broken in the willow tree that hung over the bank of the stream.

"Will, look over there," Gid said. He started toward the tree.

"Hold it, Little Brother," Will called.

Gid stopped. "What is it?"

"Don't you think there's somethin' a little strange about that? In the first place, those limbs should be supple enough not to be broken by someone passing through them. And in the second place, the two men we're tracking haven't done anything as foolish as ride through the brush before now."

"You sayin' the limbs were broken on purpose?" Gid asked.

"Yeah, that's what I'm thinkin'," Will said. At that instant, the hair pricked on the back of his neck. Someone had the drop on them. "Get down!" Will shouted.

Suddenly, and unexpectedly, Will threw himself off his horse. At almost the precise instant he made his move, a rifle boomed and a .44-40 bullet cracked through the air at exactly the place where his head had been but a second earlier.

Will and Gid hit the water feet first, then ran through the stream, splashing silver sheets of spray as they headed for the bank on the opposite side. They zigzagged as they ran and when the rifle boomed a second time, the strike of the bullet in the water demonstrated the wisdom of their erratic motion, for it too hit where, but a second earlier, one of them had been.

The two brothers dived into the tall grass on the bank of the stream, then wriggled toward the protection of a large rock about ten yards away. Though they were concealed by the grass, they weren't protected by it, and a lucky shot would be disastrous.

Will bent over a large cattail, and hooked his hat on top. He found a fairly long branch and used it to hold the cattail down while he backed away from it, moving closer to the protection offered by the boulder. When he was as far away from the cattail as the long branch would let him be, he let go and the cattail, with his hat on top, sprung back to the upright position.

Almost instantly the rifle boomed again and Will saw his hat go flying. He used that opportunity to move the last few feet to the boulder. There, he sat with his back against the rock and took a few deep breaths.

"Crockett? Are you hit?"

Will recognized Donnie Hamilton's voice.

"You weren't even close, Donnie," Will called from behind the rock.

Will heard Hamilton gasp in surprise, for not only was Will not where Hamilton expected him to be, he had also not been hit.

"You son of a bitch!" Hamilton shouted. He fired two more times in the vicinity of where he had heard Will's voice, but the bullets whistled harmlessly overhead.

"Why don't you give up, Donnie? There's no way you're going to get out of this alive."

"Give up? And go back to hang?"

Will chuckled. "I'll admit you don't have much to look forward to," he said. "But you may as well know we're taking you out of here, in your saddle or belly-down on it. Now, which is it to be?"

"Let me think about it a moment."

"Don't take too long," Will said.

There was a long moment of silence, then Hamilton called again.

"Crockett, you ever thought you 'n your brother might've followed the same trail I rode? Could be you boys was the one with a price on your heads and not me."

"Could've been," Will admitted. "Has been, in fact."

Hamilton chuckled. "I just had me an idea that you two boys has run from the law before. I mean, when you stop and think about it, we ain't all that different, are we?"

"Neither one of us has ever shot any innocent women," Gid called.

"Yeah, well, if you're talkin' about the doc's wife, it was Charley that shot her. None of the rest of us had anything to do with that."

"You didn't make any effort to stop him."

"No, I reckon we didn't," Donnie replied.

Suddenly, and unexpectedly, Will heard the sound of horses hooves, and when he raised up and looked around, he saw that Hamilton had managed to get mounted and was now galloping toward them. Hamilton had his pistol in his hand and he was firing as he rode. One bullet took a nick out of Will's hand, causing him to drop his pistol.

"See you in hell, Crockett!" Hamilton shouted, taking dead aim at Will.

From the corner of his eye, Will saw something that Hamilton didn't see. Gid had stood up from behind a rock and was pointing his pistol at Hamilton.

"Hold it, Donnie! I've got the drop on you!" Gid shouted.

Hamilton swung his pistol toward Gid and fired. Gid fired back, and Will saw a puff of dust rising from Hamilton's vest, followed by a tiny spray of blood. Hamilton pitched backward out of his saddle. One foot hung up in the stirrup, and his horse continued to run, raising a plume of water as Hamilton was dragged through the stream. As the horse tried to climb the bank out of the water, Hamilton's foot disconnected from the stirrup and he lay motionless, half in the water and half out.

Gid ran over to him, his gun still drawn. When he saw that Hamilton was unarmed, having lost his pistol during the dragging, Gid holstered his gun and pulled Hamilton the rest of the way out of the water. Will came up then, as well, and they were surprised to see that Hamilton was still breathing, though the rattle of his breathing told them that the outlaw wouldn't be alive much longer.

"That was a damn fool thing to do," Gid said.

Hamilton tried to laugh, but when he did so, bubbles of blood frothed out from the corner of his mouth.

"I reckon it was," he admitted. "But there wasn't no way I was goin' to let you two take me back to be hung. To tell the truth, I was kinda hopin' one of you would shoot me."

"Where are the others?" Will asked.

Hamilton, who had closed his eyes in pain, now opened them and looked at Will.

"You think I'm goin' to tell you that?"

"You don't owe any of them anything," Will advised him.

"Hell, Crockett, I know that," Hamilton replied. "That ain't the reason I ain't goin' to tell you boys nothin'. I ain't tellin' you nothin' 'cause it's the only way I got now of getting' at you."

"It makes no difference whether you tell us or not," Will said. "We're goin' to find them. Especially Kellett."

Again Hamilton tried to laugh, and again bubbles of blood frothed from his mouth.

"Yeah, you prob'ly will. Fact is, Kellett told me 'bout the little girl him and Alvarado raped and murdered, so I hope you do find the bastard. But if it takes you just one day longer, then I figure I'll have my laugh." Hamilton suddenly took two or three gasping breaths, then he died.

Chapter Ten

From two miles away, Will and Gid could see the little town of Dona Ana baking under the sun. It was hot, dry, dusty, and as brittle as tumbleweed. They had filled their canteens at the stream, and filled Hamilton's as well, figuring that since he was belly-down on the horse behind them, he wouldn't mind.

Even with the extra canteen they had rationed their water, but now, with the town in front of them, they let themselves drink the final few swallows. The water was warm, and their tongues were so swollen and dry that any moisture, regardless of temperature, was welcome. And, although they were drinking tepid water, they could almost taste the cool beer they would have in the saloon in town.

Will hooked his canteen back onto the saddle pommel then urged the two horses forward, the one he was riding and the one he was leading. The buildings in the town had collected the day's heat and were now giving it back in waves so that Dona Ana seemed to shimmer in the distance. A dust devil developed in front of them, propelled by a wind that felt as if it were blowing straight from the fires of hell.

"We ever been to this town before, big brother?" Gid asked.

Will shook his head. "Not that I can recall."

"Sure don't seem like much of a town."

"If it's got a saloon, it's town enough," Will said.

Gid chuckled. "You got that right."

It took the better part of a quarter hour to reach the town after they first saw it, and they rode in slowly, sizing it up with wary eyes. It was a town with only one street. The unpainted wood of the few ramshackle buildings was turning gray and splitting. There was no railroad coming into Dona Ana, but there was a stagecoach station with a schedule board announcing the arrival and departure of four stage coaches per week. Over the last several years, the two brothers had encountered many towns like this, isolated, inbred, and stagnant.

They rode past the buildings, Will subconsciously enumerating them as he passed. There was a rooming house, a livery, a smithy's, and a general store that said "Drugs, Meats, Goods" on its high, false front. There was a hotel and restaurant, too and, of course, the ubiquitous saloon ... this one called the Big Gulp Saloon. Across the street from the saloon was the jail. Will and Gid rode up to the hitching rail in front of the jail. Will dismounted and patted his shirt and pants a few times. The action sent up puffs of white dust, which hovered around him like a cloud. Gid, still mounted, looked up and down the street. A few buildings away a door slammed, while across the street, an isinglass shade came down on the upstairs window of the hotel. A sign creaked in the wind and flies buzzed loudly around the piles of horse manure that lay in the street.

"You stay out here and keep your eyes open," Will said. "I'll see if I can cash Mr. Hamilton in."

Gid nodded.

Will pushed open the door. No one was at the desk, but someone was sleeping in a bunk in one of the cells. The door to that cell, like the door to all of them, was standing open. Except for this one, all the cells were empty.

Will walked over to the wall where several posters were tacked and began studying them. He had left the door to the building standing open, and a gust of wind blew it shut with a loud bang.

"What? What?" the man in the cell said, awakened by the sound. He sat up on the bunk and saw Will standing by his poster wall.

"Who are you?" he asked.

Will looked toward him. "You a prisoner?" he asked.

"A prisoner? Hell no I'm not a prisoner," the man said indignantly. "I'm the sheriff, by damn!"

"I got a body for you," Will said.

"A body? Where?"

"Belly-down across his horse," Will said. "He's tied up out front."

"Who is it?"

Will saw a poster with Donnie Hamilton's name and picture, and he tore it down. "This man," he said.

The sheriff, who was bald-headed and overweight, came out of the cell stuffing his shirt down into his trousers. "The hell you say. Donnie Hamilton, huh? He's a bad one. Did you kill him?"

"My brother did. He's outside with the body."

"I suppose you'll be puttin' in for the reward?"

Will glared at the sheriff. "We didn't kill him for the sport of it," he said.

"No, I don't reckon you did. Well, let me take a look at him and I'll send a wire back," the sheriff said, starting toward the door. "Who will I say is putting in for the reward?"

"Crockett. Will and Gid Crockett."

"Crockett?" the sheriff replied. He stared hard at Will. "You two is actually the Crockett Brothers?"

"That's what we're called," Will said. He nodded toward the posters. "Has Charley Kellett been through here?"

"I wouldn't know if he has or not," the sheriff answered. "But in truth, even if I seen 'im, I'd give 'im a wide berth. The only job I got is to keep the peace in Dona Ana. I ain't in the man huntin' business. Once I get confirmation to pay you, where will I find you?"

"Soon as we board our horses, we'll be in the saloon just down the street," Will said.

News of the Crocketts bringing in Donnie Hamilton reached the saloon before the two brothers did, so that everyone was talking about them, even before they arrived. Ralph Hopkins overheard the talk as he was eating beans at a table in the back of the saloon. He was planning to leave Dona Ana that night, to join up with Charley Kellett, and he thought this might be some information Kellett would want to know.

"Here they come!" someone hissed, and the saloon grew quiet. A moment later, Will and Gid Crockett pushed their way through the bat-wing doors.

Hopkins got an idea. He wasn't sure how good an idea it was ... there was no one with him he could ask about it. But it was an idea he couldn't shake, and, if he could pull it off, he knew it would go down well with Charley Kellett.

The Crocketts didn't know him and wouldn't be expecting anything. Hopkins was good with both a gun and a knife. He was fast, and he was accurate. Everyone told him that. If he just opened up on the two brothers, he was sure he could get them before they got him. In fact, if he used his knife, he might be able to get one of them before the other one even realized he was in danger.

"Give us each a beer," he heard one of them say to the bartender.

The bartender drew the beers and put them on the bar. The bigger of the two brothers, the one Hopkins knew was Gid, blew off the head then drank nearly three-quarters of it before he put it down. Then he wiped his mouth with the back of his hand and turned his back to the bar to look out over the patrons.

Damn! He's looking right at me! Hopkins thought. No, he couldn't be. He was just looking around the room, that's all. There was no way the Crocketts could know about him.

Gid looked right toward Hopkins, then passed his eyes around the rest of the room.

If Hopkins was going to get them, he would never have a better chance than now.

Gid finished the beer, then turned toward the barkeep to ask for another when suddenly something flashed by in front of him. It was a knife! The blade buried itself about half an inch into the bar with a solid thunk. After that, the handle vibrated back and forth.

Will had also seen the knife coming, and even as the knife was burying itself in the bar, Will had his pistol out and was turning toward the direction from which the knife had come. He saw a man getting up from a table with a gun in his hand. However, when that man saw how quickly Will had drawn, he held his hands up, letting the pistol dangle from its trigger guard.

"No, no," he shouted. "Don't shoot, me, mister. Don't shoot!"

"Why the hell not?" Will growled. "If you would've had your way, my brother would be wearing that Arkansas toothpick by now." Will squinted at Hopkins. "What'd you do that for? We ever run across each other before?"

"No," Hopkins admitted.

"Then why did you try to kill me?" Gid asked.

"Could be I just don't like your looks," Hopkins said.

"That's not much of a reason for killing a man," Gid said.

"I've kilt men for less reason. You have, too, I reckon, from what I've heared about you."

"What have you heard of us?"

"I've heard that there's people will pay good money to see you dead."

"Could be," Will admitted. "But you won't be collecting any of it. Drop your gun."

Hopkins made no move to drop his gun.

"Drop it, I said, or I'll kill you where you stand," Will said, menacingly.

Hopkins smiled, then slowly turned the pistol around so that the butt was pointing toward Will.

"You ain't goin' to shoot me," he said. "I've done give up, and this here saloon is full of witnesses who'll swear I was handin' you my gun. You shoot me now, you'll hang."

"Go ahead and shoot the son of a bitch, anyway," Gid said. "We haven't been hanged yet, and there's been a heap of people try."

Will stared at Hopkins, and for a long moment it looked as if he might actually do it. Then he sighed. "I should do what my brother says. But I'm feeling generous, so I think I'll just take you across the street and throw you in jail until we leave. If you're real nice to the sheriff, he might feed you."

"You ain't scarin' me none, Crockett. I don't mind coolin' my heels here for a while. You goin' to take my gun or ain't you?"

Will started across the floor for Hopkins's gun, but before he had gone half a step, Hopkins executed as neat a border roll as Will had ever seen. Will wasn't often caught by surprise, but this time he was. Not only by the fact that Hopkins would try such a thing, but by the skill with which Hopkins was able to do it.

Gid was standing by the bar without a pistol in his hand, and Will had relaxed his own position to the point where he had actually let the hammer down, and even lowered the gun. Now he had to raise his pistol back into line while at the same time cocking it. And he was slowed by the fact that he first had to react to Hopkins's action.

The quiet room was suddenly shattered with the roar of two pistols snapping firing caps and exploding powder almost simultaneously. The bar patrons yelled and dived or scrambled for cover. White gun smoke billowed out in a cloud that filled the center of the room, momentarily obscuring everything.

As the smoke began to clear, Hopkins stared through the white cloud, smiling broadly at Will. He opened his mouth as if to speak. The only sound he made, however, was a gagging rattle, way back in his throat. The smile left his face, his eyes glazed over, and he pitched forward, his gun clattering to the floor.

Will stood ready to fire a second time if needed, but a second shot wasn't necessary. He looked down at Hopkins for a moment, then holstered his pistol.

There were calls from outside, then the sound of people running. Several came into the saloon and stood under the rising cloud of gun smoke to stare in wonder at the dead man on the floor. One of the new arrivals was the sheriff.

"Damn me if death don't seem to follow you Crockett boys like a black cloud," the sheriff observed. He pointed at the body on the floor. "I take it, this is your doin'?"

"Yes," Will answered. "I had no choice, you can ask anyone."

"That's right, Sheriff, this here fella shot first," someone said.

The sheriff nodded. "He one of the ones you're after?"

Will shook his head. "Hell, I don't even know who the son of a bitch is."

"His name is Hopkins. Ralph Hopkins," the sheriff said.

"You know him?"

The sheriff nodded. "He's been hanging around town for the last two or three months. Pretty much of a bully, but I haven't had any trouble with him before."

"Ralph Hopkins? I don't recognize his name. Is there paper on him, too?"

"I'm not sure," the sheriff replied. "I just sent the wire about Donnie Hamilton. I reckon I can send another one askin' about Hopkins."

"I'm obliged. I didn't set out to cash him in, but if he's worth anything, I might as well take it."

"What about the body?" the sheriff asked.

Will shrugged. "That's your department now,

sheriff. I'm turning him over to you. Put him alongside Hamilton. They're birds of a feather." As Will talked to the sheriff, he knelt beside Hopkins's body and began going through the outlaw's pockets.

"I thought you said the body was mine," the sheriff said.

"The body is yours," Will replied. "What I find in his pockets is mine. Anyway, you haven't signed the receipt yet."

Will found a money clip containing twenty dollars in paperback currency. In addition to the paper money, there were fifteen dollars in coin. He handed the coin to the sheriff. "You can use this to bury him," he said.

"Thanks," the sheriff replied, putting the coins in his pocket.

Will looked up at the bartender. "You ever know Hopkins to buy anyone a drink?"

"No," the bartender answered. "He was a tight son of a bitch."

Will gave the twenty dollars in paper to the barkeep. "Well, he's buyin' drinks now. Set 'em up as long as the money lasts."

The bartender smiled broadly. "Yes, sir," he said. "Boys, the drinks are on Hopkins!" he called.

After Hopkins's body was dragged out of the saloon and the excitement of the event had died down, Will and Gid sat at the same table where Hopkins had been sitting and ordered a meal of bacon, eggs, and coffee.

Back in the kitchen, Gid saw a boy sweeping the floor and motioned to him. When the boy came out to the table, Gid gave him a coin and asked him to take care of their horses. Their supper had just been put before them when the boy returned.

"I put up your horses, mister," the boy said.

"Thanks."

"Was he a bad man? The one that was killed?"

"Yes," Gid replied.

The boy smiled. "I thought he was. I could tell."

"How could you tell?"

"His eyes," the boy said, moving his fingers across his own eyes. "They were evil. His smile was not happy. He drank a lot and kept watching the door."

"He kept watching the door, you say?" Will asked.

"Yes, sir."

"Thanks. You have a good eye."

The boy smiled proudly. "Someday soon I'm going to leave Dona Ana and become a great gunfighter, just like you," he said.

"Your mother and dad may want you to wait until you're a little older."

"I have no parents," the boy said.

"Where do you live?"

"Mr. Zeller lets me stay in a room in the stable and don't charge me nothing 'cause I muck out the stalls for him. Mr. Elam, who owns this saloon, gives me three meals a day because I sweep the floors for him. I have a good life."

Will smiled. "I guess you do at that," he said.

Chapter Eleven

Will and Gid had taken rooms in the front of the hotel. The next morning a series of loud popping noises woke Will from the soundest sleep he had enjoyed in days. Startled, he sat straight up in bed, slipped his pistol from the holster, which hung from the bedpost, then got to his feet, ready for any intrusion. There was another series of loud pops, followed by the high peal of a woman's laughter, then the sound of a brass band.

Will moved over to the window and pulled the curtain to one side as he looked down on the street. The street was full of men and women, all dressed in their most colorful finery. There seemed to be a parade of some sort in progress, led by the brass band and a troupe of acrobatic dancers, followed by a highly polished, brass fire-engine pumper. The smell of food cooking over open fires filled the soft morning air and Will decided he would go down to have breakfast and to see what was going on.

When he got downstairs, he saw Gid eating a sandwich of barbequed beef and biscuit as he watched the celebration.

"I see you found the food," Will said.

Gid held up the biscuit. "This isn't bad. You ought to try it."

"Maybe I will," Will said, heading toward a stand that was selling sandwiches.

Smiling broadly, the sheriff came up to the two brothers then. "You'll like our barbeque," he said. "Folks from all over talk about how good Dona Ana barbeque is."

"I haven't been keeping up with the date," Will said. "What's the occasion? Is it the Fourth of July?"

The sheriff laughed. "Fourth of July? Nope."

"Then what's the celebration?" he asked.

"Why, you and your brother are the cause of our celebration," the sheriff replied. "You mean you haven't figured that out yet?"

"What the hell are you talking about? How are we the cause of your celebration?"

"I take it you haven't gone down to look at the display on the porch of the general store," the sheriff said.

"No."

"Maybe you should. I think you will be proud."

Finishing their sandwiches, the two boys walked

down toward the general store. There were men, women, and children standing around the front porch looking at whatever it was the sheriff said was displayed there.

"I'll be damned," Gid said when they were close enough to see the display.

There, in a pair of wooden coffins standing up against the wall, were the bodies of Donnie Hamilton and Ralph Hopkins. Though probably neither outlaw had ever worn a suit in his life, they were both wearing new black suits in death. Their arms were crossed across their chest. Donnie Hamilton was holding a pistol in his right hand and nothing in his left. Hopkins clutched a pistol in his left hand and the knife he had thrown at Gid in his right. Hamilton's eyes were closed, but Hopkins's were open, though the lid of his left eye was drooped half-closed. Hopkins's mouth was closed, but Hamilton's mouth was open in what was almost a sardonic smile.

"It's the Crockett brothers!" someone shouted, noticing Will and Gid looking at the bodies.

"The Crocketts!"

"Three cheers for the Crocketts!" someone else called. "Hip, hip..."

"Hooray!"

"Hip, hip..."

"Hooray!"

"Hip, hip..."

"Hooray!"

Will held up his hand to silence them, then walked up for a closer look at a hand-lettered sign propped up at the foot of the coffins:

Here are the bodies of the bandits
Donnie Hamilton and Ralph Hopkins, killed by
Will and Gid Crockett
The gunfights that killed the two men took place
right here in Dona Ana

"This is going to make our town very famous," someone said, and when Gid looked around, he saw the young boy who had stabled his horse for him the night before. "Of course, everyone knows that Donnie Hamilton wasn't really killed here, but we have his body, and the sheriff says that's the same thing."

"Is that what everyone thinks?" Gid asked. "That this is going to make Dona Ana famous?"

"Yes," the boy answered. "The sheriff said that now everyone will come to see where the gunfights happened. They'll buy drinks and meals in the saloon and they'll stay in the hotel. The sheriff says everyone will get rich because of this."

"And that's what all this is about? This parade and picnic?"

"Yes," the boy replied. "The sheriff says we'll have such a celebration every year at this time. It'd be nice if you could come every year."

"Sure. And maybe we could kill someone new for you next year," Will suggested.

"Do you think so? That would really be good," the boy said enthusiastically, not picking up on Will's sarcasm.

Will shook his head slowly, then nodded at his brother.

"Let's go," he said. "The sooner we get out of this town, the better."

"For you boys, there's no charge," the liveryman said when Will and Gid reclaimed their horses. "You've made our town famous."

"And so, out of a sense of civic duty, you boarded our horses free?" Will asked.

The liveryman looked around, then said in a quieter voice, "Yes, but also I have taken Donnie Hamilton's horse. It will more than pay the bill."

"Yes, I'm sure it would," Gid said as the two brothers mounted and rode away.

There had been reaction to their killing before, especially during the war when they were able to extract vengeance for some of the more heinous atrocities. But never before had an entire town put their victims on public display and thrown a town party to celebrate. It was more than the boys could stomach, and they couldn't wait to shake the dust of this town from their feet. As soon as they reached the outer limits of town, they urged their horses into a trot, putting as much distance behind them as they could.

Chapter Twelve

Charley Kellett tried to piss a grasshopper off a weed, but wasn't successful. He buttoned his trousers, then walked back over to the remains of the camp where he and Moody had spent the night. There was a small pile of blackened twigs from the fire they had built the night before.

"You sure you told Hopkins where to meet us?" Moody asked.

"Yeah," Kellett answered with a growl. "I told him."

"He's late."

"He's not late," Kellett said. "The dumb bastard isn't showing up. Hell, I should've known better than to count on him anyway."

"So, what do we do now?" Moody asked.

"We'll pull the job by ourselves."

"You think we can do it? I mean, with just the two

of us?" Moody asked.

"Why the hell not?" Kellett replied. "Besides, this way, there'll be more money for us."

"Yeah," Moody said, smiling broadly. "Yeah, that's right, ain't it?"

"Let's go," Kellett said, walking toward the horses they had already saddled.

Crawford was a small town, just as Kellett had said. However, it was a busy town, and a half dozen wagons were parked along the streets. The board sidewalks were full of men, women, farmers, and ranchers, looking in the windows of the shops, hurrying to and fro.

"What the hell?" Moody asked, surprised by the number of people. "Is this Saturday?"

"How the hell do I know? I don't keep no damn calendar," Kellett responded with a growl.

"Seems to me like they's a awful lot of people in town, Charley," Moody said. "Maybe too many."

"Yeah?" Kellett answered. "Well, look at 'em. Most of 'em ain't even wearin' guns. Don't worry about it."

"That looks like the bank over there," Moody said, pointing to a rather flimsy-looking building. It was thrown together from rip-sawed lumber, and it was leaning so that it looked as if a good, stiff wind could knock it over.

"Hell, we don't have to rob this bank," Kellett said.

"We can just kick the walls in."

"Let's do it and be gone," Moody suggested.

"Wait a minute, wait a minute," Kellett said, holding up his hand. "Let's take a ride up and down the street first, just to get our bearings."

"What do you have in mind?"

"We'll ride down to the far end of the street and back. You take the left side. Count ever' body you see carryin' a gun. I'll take the right."

The two men rode slowly down the entire length of the town, then they turned their horses and rode back.

"I seen three that was wearing guns," Moody said.

"I only seen one on my side," Kellett said. "What about the three you seen? Any of 'em look like they know how to use 'em?" Kellett asked.

Moody laughed. "Nah. One old fart didn't look like he had the strength to even pull his gun out of the holster, let alone use it."

"Well, then, what do you say we get us a little travelin' money?"

Kellett and Moody swung down from their horses, then wrapped the reins loosely over the hitching rail.

As soon as the two men were inside, they pulled their pistols.

"This is a holdup!" Kellett shouted. "You, teller, empty out your bank drawer and put all the money in a bag!"

Nervously, the teller began to comply, emptying his drawer in just a few seconds.

"Is that all there is? There can't be more'n a couple hundred there," Kellett said in disbelief.

"That's all there is," the teller insisted.

Kellett took the sack. "I want to see what you've got in the safe," he demanded.

"The hell you are! I just put my money in this bank, mister, and you ain't getting' a cent of it!" a customer suddenly shouted. Kellett swung his gun toward the customer, who was also armed. The customer fired first. His bullet hit an inkwell on one of the tables, sending up a black spray of ink. Kellett returned fire, and his bullet found its mark. Moody fired toward the teller's window, and his bullet shattered the shaded glass around the teller cages.

"Let's get the hell out of here!" Kellett shouted.

Outside the bank the townspeople, hearing the shots, realized at once what was going on.

"The bank!" someone shouted. "They're robbin' the bank!"

One of the armed townspeople started running toward the bank with his pistol drawn. Moody, who was the first one out of the bank, shot him, dropping him in the middle of the street. Seeing that, the townspeople began screaming and running for cover.

Clutching the canvas bag in his left hand, Kellett

fired three more shots into the bank, knocking out the windows on both sides and in the door.

"Hurry! Get mounted!" Moody called, holding the reins down for Kellett.

Across the street a young store clerk, no more than a boy, came running out of the store, wearing his apron and carrying a broom in one hand and a rifle in the other. He dropped the broom, raised the rifle, and fired. His shot hit Moody in the side, and, with a roar of pain and anger, Moody fired back, killing the boy.

From the front porch of a hardware store, a man fired both barrels of a shotgun, but his gun was loaded with light birdshot and he was too far away to be effective. The pellets peppered and stung, but none of them penetrated the skin.

Another citizen had better luck, in that his bullet killed Kellett's horse. Kellett, with the bag of money in his hand, leaped from the saddle as his animal went down, then ran toward the nearest hitch rail. There, several horses were tied, left by their owners who had come into town. The horses were spooked by all the gunfire and they reared and pulled against their restraints.

Kellett grabbed the horse nearest him and swung into the saddle. When the owner stepped out the door of a nearby shop to protest, Kellett shot at him, and the bullet, hitting the door frame right beside the owner's head, drove him back inside.

The sheriff, an older man, just as Kellett had described him, was now reaching the scene, having run the entire length of the street from the sheriff's office. He was carrying a rifle, and he raised it to his shoulders.

"You fellas stop right there!" he called.

"Would you look at that old fool?" Kellett said. He dropped the sheriff with a shot to the chest.

The two outlaws rode toward the end of town only to see a dozen or more of the townspeople rolling a wagon into the street. The townspeople then tipped the wagon over as a barricade and gathered behind it, all of them armed and ready.

"Charley, we can't go that way!" Moody shouted.

"This way!" Kellett yelled, turning off the street and leading them through a churchyard where a grave was being dug.

At the sound of gunfire and the sight of mounted and armed men bearing down on them, the grave diggers jumped into the hole they were digging. The two horses cleared the hole and were off.

By the time the townspeople were able to regroup and get mounted, Kellett and Moody had a two-mile lead on them. With the sheriff dead and no effective leader to organize them, the pursuit only lasted for a few miles. After that, the men gave up and came back to town to help calm the fears and bury the dead.

"They've stopped chasin' us," Kellett said, looking back over his shoulder. "We can give the animals a blow now."

They reined up, then swung down from their saddles and began walking their horses. Moody, who had been hit in the hip, was walking with a painful limp. There was blood on the front of his trousers.

"You bad hit, Jasper?" Kellett asked solicitously.

"No."

"You sure? You're covered with blood and you got a pretty bad hitch-along in your get-about there."

"I ain't hurt bad," Moody insisted. "I got a bullet in my hip, but it didn't hit none of my vitals."

"Yeah, well, we can't leave the bullet in there," Kellett said. "We'll have to get you to a doctor somewhere."

"No!" Moody shouted. "I seen how you got a doctor for Wagner. I ain't plannin' on lettin' you leave me somewhere to die."

"That was different," Charley said. "We was on the run then."

"Well, what the hell, Charley? We ain't exactly goin' to a picnic now."

Kellett laughed. "That's the truth," he said. "All right, if you think you can keep up, come ahead. But you start slowin' me down any, I'm goin' to leave you.'

"I didn't figure it would be any otherwise," Moody replied.

"If you want, I can get that bullet out for you," Kellett offered.

"You a doctor, are you?"

"I've took out a few bullets in my day," Kellett said. "And some of 'em lived."

"I'll pass on that offer, but thanks just the same," Moody said.

Despite Moody's brave protestations, by nightfall the pain was almost unbearable, and he knew he wouldn't be able to go on unless the bullet was removed. He finally spoke the words.

"Charley," he said thickly. "You serious 'bout bein' able to take out a bullet?"

Kellett chuckled. "You ready for it to come out now, are you?"

"Yes."

"I thought you would be. I've heard 'em talk brave before, but most always they change their mind. I'll take it out for you."

"Thanks."

"It's goin' to cost you."

"Cost me? Cost me what?"

"Your share of the money we took from the bank."

"Are you crazy? I got shot for that money. You think

I'm goin' to give it to you?"

"Don't look to me like you got no choice," Kellett said. "Anyhow, what's the big deal? We only got a little over two-hundred dollars. Your share's just a hundred bucks."

"Who would've thought they'd put up such a fight for just two-hundred dollars?" Moody asked.

"Do we have a deal?" Kellett asked.

At that very moment a wave of nauseating pain swept over Moody with such intensity that it was all he could do to stay in the saddle.

"All right, you bastard, all right, we have a deal. You can have my share, just get the damn bullet out," Moody said in a strained voice.

"I know this country," Kellett said. "We'll head up into that draw over there. That'll take us into Rattlesnake Canyon. Maybe we can hole up for a while."

"We're goin' to hole up?" Moody asked.

"That's right, Jasper, we're goin' to hole up," Kellett said. He chuckled. "Did you really think I was goin' to leave you?"

"I don't know," Moody answered. "Yeah, I guess I thought you might."

"Well, I ain't. You an' me are the only ones left now. That means we got to stick together. Besides, what would folks think of Kansas Charley if they knew he abandoned his friends?"

"Yeah," Moody replied, thinking of Frank Wagner, Perry Hoyt, and Donnie Hamilton. "What would they think of you."

It was another hour of painful riding before they stopped. Moody climbed down from his horse, removed the saddle, then lay down, using it as a pillow. The pain which had been localized in his hip now spread throughout both legs and up his back.

"You need to build us a fire," Moody said.

"Kind of hate to," Kellett replied. "You can see a fire a long way off at night. Somebody might see this and get to wonderin' who's out here."

"You've got to have a fire so's you can heat the knife," Moody said.

"All right, I'll build a little one," Kellett agreed.

Moody, no longer having to fight to stay in the saddle, drifted in and out of consciousness. He was aware of Kellett gathering bits of mesquite wood, but he didn't see him actually start the fire. A few moments later, though, he did see the golden bubble of light in the night, with Kellett silhouetted against the flames.

Then he passed out again.

He woke up again when Kellett started actually digging for the bullet. The pain was excruciating, much more intense than it had been at any time before. He passed out again. When he came to the next time,

Kellett was holding the bloodied bullet between his fingers and smiling broadly, his eyes and teeth glowing orange-red in the snapping fire.

"Can you believe this?" Kellett said. "This here's a .22. Who shot you anyway, Jasper? Some kid with a toy gun?"

"I don't remember," Moody replied, though, at that moment, he did recall that he had killed a young, apron-clad boy.

"Give me three of your bullets," Kellett said.

"What? What do you want my bullets for?"

"Because I need the gunpowder," Kellett replied. "And I ain't plannin' on usin' any of my own."

"I got a box of cartridges in my saddlebag," Moody said. He tried to reach for them but was too weak.

"I'll get 'em," Kellett offered generously. When he opened the box he took out ten or twelve, dropping the extra cartridges into his own pocket. He came back to sit beside Moody as he separated the bullets from the cartridges. When he had all three separated, he poured the powder on the wound.

"What's that for?" Moody asked.

"You'll see," Kellett replied. Without a word of explanation, he picked up a burning brand from the fire and touched off the powder. It made a white-hot flash.

Moody had time only for a gasp of pain before he passed out.

Chapter Thirteen

When Moody opened his eyes the next morning, he was looking directly at the campfire, or rather, at what had been the campfire. Now there were only a few white coals with a tiny wisp of smoke curling up from the ashes.

"Charley," he said. "Charley, could I have a drink of water?"

When no one answered, Moody turned, with a great effort, to look around. He didn't see anyone.

"Charley?" he shouted, the effort of the yell causing his wound to throb.

There was still no answer.

With a supreme effort, Moody sat up and looked around. The camp was totally deserted. Not only was Kellett gone, but so were the horses. Kellett had left in the night, leaving Moody wounded and without a mount.

"You son of a bitch!" Moody shouted. "You bastard!"

ROBERT VAUGHAN

He picked up a rock and threw it, though the effort caused pain to shoot through him like a hot knife. He fell back down and lay there until the pain subsided somewhat. The thirst he had awakened with seemed to increase with his efforts, so he reached for his canteen. When he couldn't find it on his saddle pommel, he looked around for it.

The canteen was gone. So were his saddlebags. There had been jerky, raisins, and dried beans in there. Kellett had taken his food and water as well.

Waves of panic swept over him, pushing aside the rage and even the pain. He was abandoned out there, no horse, too wounded to walk, and no food or water. He was going to die a long, slow, agonizing death. Even Frank Wagner had it better than this, he thought. He had food, water, and a place to sleep, followed by a quick death.

"Shit!" he shouted into the dry, morning wind. "I would have been better off lettin' 'em hang me."

Moody saw his pistol and, in a sudden impulse, drew it from his holster. He put the barrel to his temple.

"Charley Kellett!" he shouted. "I'll be waiting for you in hell!"

He pulled the trigger.

At about that same moment, Will and Gid were pushing through the bat-wing doors of the Redeye Saloon in the little town of Good Bend Crossing. Because it was a little early for the saloon's trade, it was relatively quiet. An empty beer mug and a half-full ashtray were placed conveniently by the piano to provide the only evidence that anyone ever played the instrument.

The boys ordered beer, and when it was served, Will turned around to survey the room as he drank it.

Two people were sitting at the table nearest the piano ... a middle-aged cowboy and the only bar girl who was working at this hour. The fact that both of them had only one glass before them, and that the glass was still half-full, indicated that the bar girl either found the cowboy's company pleasant, or had accepted the slowness of the hour.

There were a few people sitting at one of the other tables as well, and a lively card game was in progress. The table was crowded with brightly colored poker chips and empty beer mugs. There were two brass spittoons within spitting distance of the players, but despite their presence, the floor was riddled with expectorated tobacco quids and chewed cigar butts.

Suddenly one of the players threw his cards on the table in disgust, then stood up. "I've had it, boys," he said. "I ain't drawed a winnin' hand since I sat down."

One of the players looked over toward the bar and saw Will watching them.

"We have an empty chair here, mister, if you'd

care to sit in."

Will looked at Gid.

"Go ahead," Gid said. "Hell, you never have been able to resist a good poker game."

Will tossed the rest of his drink down, then wiped the back of his hand across his mouth. Gid was right when he said Will enjoyed a poker game. But he also knew that it was sometimes easier to pick up information through casual conversation over a few drinks and a deck of cards than to ask outright. Maybe someone at the table had heard something about Kellett.

"Thanks for the invite," Will said. "I reckon I will join you if you don't mind."

"What you take out of your pocket and put in front of you is all the money you can play with," one of the men said. "You can't go back for more."

"And you can't put anymore in front of you than the most any one of us has showing," another added.

"Sounds fair," Will said, looking around the table. "Who's been the winner so far?"

"That'd be the doc, here," one of the cowboys said. "You'd better watch out for him. He's pretty good at the game."

"Thanks for the warning. And you would be the doc?" Will asked, addressing the man with the largest pile of money.

"I am," the tall, thin, cadaverous-looking man replied. He was wearing a black suit, a shoestring tie, and a flat crown black hat. He counted the money in front of him. "I've got forty-five dollars here."

Will bought forty-five dollars' worth of chips and stacked them up in front of him.

"You two boys just passin' through Good Bend Crossing?" the man in black asked as he dealt the cards. It was easy to see why he was ahead. He handled the cards easily, gracefully, whereas the others around the table looked awkward even picking up the pasteboards.

"My brother is," Will answered, nodding toward Gid, who had just ordered a second beer. "But for me, it depends."

"On what?" one of the other men asked, curious about Will's comment.

"It depends on how much I win here," Will answered. "If I win enough money, I might just settle down, right here in Good Bend Crossing. I'll buy a ranch and some cattle, get married, raise a family, join a church, run for the city council, and become a substantial citizen."

The men around the table laughed out loud.

"Say, Smokey," Doc called to the cowboy who was sitting with the bar girl. "Did you hear this fella? If he wins big, he's goin' to be lookin' for a wife. You better hang on to Maggie while you can."

Maggie looked over at Will. "Honey, you're a good lookin' man," she teased. "You wouldn't have to win too much to get me."

Maggie's good-natured response brought more laughter.

Will won the first hand.

"Better watch it, Doc," one of the cowboys said. "This fella's on his way."

The game continued for several hands. Will was winning a little more than he was losing, but he wasn't the big winner. But neither was Doc. Will's entrance into the game seemed somehow to change the dynamics so that everyone's luck improved slightly. That had the effect of improving the corporate mood, and the talk came freely.

Besides Dr. Eastman, who was a real doctor in addition to being an almost professional gambler, the other men in the game were Neil Davis, a small rancher, Dudley Steward, a gunsmith, and Al Cotoggio, who owned the feed and seed store.

"Say," Will said as if merely taking part in the conversation, "did any of you fellas hear about the big jailbreak they had over in Bonito a few weeks ago?"

"Jailbreak? Mister, that's old news. Where you been?" Neil replied. "Hell, yesterday, Charley Kellett and another man robbed 'em a bank over in Crawford."

"Some bank robbery," Dudley said in disgust. "They

only made off with two hundred dollars."

"They didn't get much money, that's true," Al agreed. "But they killed some folks doin' it. And one of 'em was just a boy."

"A boy?" Doc asked. "What boy? I've doctored a few of the young'uns over there."

"It was Muley Jones' boy," Al replied. "Muley runs the general store there, you know, and his boy was workin' for him. Seems the boy had just got hisself a new .22 rifle, an' when all the shootin' started, why he run out onto the front porch an' joined in the melee. They say he hit one of 'em, though they might just be sayin' that to ease Muley's pain some. Whether he actual did hit one of 'em or not, he got their attention, 'cause he was shot dead right there on the front porch of his pa's store."

"That's a damned shame. It's too bad they didn't get all them fellas hung when they had the chance," Dudley said. "I wonder where they are now?"

"Say, you know I was talkin' to one of my night-hawks just 'afore sunup this mornin'," Neil said. "Well, it was Philip Burch. You fellas all know him. Anyhow, I was talkin' to him an' he said that last night he thought he saw a campfire down in Rattlesnake Canyon. I didn't put much store in it at the time, but now that I think back on it, don't it seem to you a little curious? I mean why would anyone want to go in there? The place is so desolate that a hawk has to carry a lunch just to fly over."

The others laughed.

"Rattlesnake Canyon, eh?" Dudley said. "You think maybe Kellett is holed up there?"

"Well, if I was on the run, that's sure where I'd go," Neil said. "Why, they's draws and gullies enough in that place to hide a whole army."

Over at the bar, Gid listened with half an ear to the dialogue going on around the table, while carrying on a simultaneous conversation with the bartender. At the same time, he was keeping an eye on Maggie and the cowboy she was drinking with. He wanted to get closer to Maggie, but he didn't want to move in on the cowboy. After a few more minutes the cowboy stood up, nodded to Maggie, then stepped over to the bar.

"I reckon she's all yours, mister," he said.

"I don't want to rush you," Gid replied.

"Hell, mister, if I stayed all night, I couldn't do no more'n look at her over a half-empty glass. Maggie's a nice girl, but she's a workin' girl, if you know what I mean."

"I know what you mean," Gid said. Gid turned to the bartender. "Give my friend here a beer, and send another drink over to the lady's table."

The cowboy smiled, broadly. "Mister, you're all right in my book."

Gid walked over to Maggie's table. "Would you like

some company?" he asked, pulling out the chair.

"Do you really want to sit here?" Maggie asked. She leaned forward, showing a generous spill of her breasts. "Or, would you rather go to where it is more comfortable?"

"You know of such a place?"

Maggie raised her eyes, glancing toward the second floor. "I have a nice room up there," she said. "If you are interested. And ... if you can afford it," she added.

Gid chuckled. "I'm interested, and I can afford it," he said, offering her his arm.

With a broad smile, Maggie stood up and stuck her arm through his.

"Cal!" Maggie called, holding her hand out toward the bartender as they walked by the corner of the bar. The one word was all she needed. Knowing what she wanted, Cal handed her a full bottle.

"Maggie, you're my kind of girl," Gid said as they started up the stairs arm in arm.

As they went up the stairs, they passed one of the girls who was coming down, just then starting her workday.

"Suzie, do me a favor and have a drink with Smokey, will you?" Maggie asked. "He's a little blue tonight."

"What's Smokey got to be blue about?"

"His dog died."

Suzie looked sad. "Oh, that's a shame. I know what a store he set by that dog."

Gid looked back down toward the bar and at the old cowboy. Smokey was carefully nursing the beer Gid had bought for him.

"Here," Gid said, taking out a couple of dollars. "Sit with him as long as this lasts."

Suzie smiled and took the money. "You'e got a deal, mister," she said.

Upstairs, Maggie unlocked the door to her room, then pushed it open. Gid looked around. It was a typical whore's room, decorated in a way that combined the fact that it was both the whore's home and her place of business. The bedcover was white with a great red heart in the middle.

"Nice," Gid said, indicating the bedspread.

"Thanks. I made it myself," Maggie replied. "But, I didn't know you come up here to talk quiltin'."

"Oh, I think we can do more than talk," Gid said with a broad smile.

The saloon, which had been fairly quiet when Gid and Maggie climbed the stairs, was beginning to fill up. It was crowded and noisy. Three of the most noticeable of the newly arrived customers were young men who wore their guns strapped low. They were louder and more boisterous than anyone else in the establishment, and they made a place for themselves at the bar by elbowing others out of the way. Occasionally one of them would get off a joke at someone else's expense, and he and the two with him would laugh uproariously at his cleverness, unaware or unconcerned that the rest of the people in the saloon were not laughing with them, but were instead taking it all in, in embarrassed silence.

"Who are the funny boys?" Will asked Neil.

"The one with blond hair and the loudest mouth is Bernie Yates. He's the oldest. The one with the red hair is Jake Hillis. The one with the dark hair and mustache is Sam Rhodes. They rode for me once, 'til I got rid of 'em. Then they rode for one rancher after another 'til, one by one ever'one got sick of 'em. I guess they been fired by near 'bout ever' spread within fifty miles. Now they mostly drift about, rounding up a few strays for their money."

"Yeah, and sometimes the strays haven't even strayed off yet," Doc said. "What gets me is why none of the ranchers know that."

"We know it," Neil admitted. "But we figure payin' a few bucks to get our strays back, is better' n havin' 'em rustled."

"They're a rowdy bunch of bullies, all right," Doc said. "Nobody likes 'em. In fact, I'm a little surprised to see them. They got drunk here two, maybe three weeks ago and tore up the place. Sheriff Lacy told them they were either goin' to have to pay for the damages or spend thirty days in jail."

"Which did they do?" Al asked.

"Hell, they didn't do either one," Doc replied. "They just lit out. This is the first time they've been back since."

"I wonder if the sheriff knows they're in town?" Dudley asked.

The three men, perhaps sensing that they were the subject of conversation, left the bar and wandered over to the card game.

"Well, now, this here looks like a friendly game," the one called Bernie said. "Any of you 'bout ready to give up your seats?"

No one answered.

"Hey, you," Bernie said to Will. Jake and Sam laughed. "Why don't you take a rest for a while and let one of us sit in the game?"

"Hey, Bernie, you want to play cards you go right ahead," Jake said. "But I didn't come into town to play no cards. Hell, we can do that out at the bunkhouse. I come for somethin' else."

"Yeah, Jake, we know what you come for," Sam said. "You come to dip your wick."

The three men found that enormously funny.

"So, how 'bout it. You goin' to get up, or what?" Jake asked.

"I'm not ready to quit yet," Will said.

"Is that so? Well, maybe if you'd win one big hand, you'd be ready," Bernie suggested. "I'll help you." He started walking around the table. "Doc, here, has hisself a pair of jacks," he said. "Neil is holdin' a king, queen, and ace, but no pair. Al has a pair of tens." He stepped behind the gunsmith's chair. "Whooowee. Now, Dudley has two kings." Bernie looked up. "Hope you can beat two kings."

Doc, Neil, Al, and Dudley groaned, and Will laid his cards faceup on the table. He had two Aces. "What do you say we leave the pot and deal again?" he suggested to the others.

"Thanks. That's damned decent of you," Doc said.

"Hold it now. That's no way to be. I'm just trying to help."

Will glared at the young cowboy. "I've had about a belly full of you, mister," he said. "Back away from the table."

Will's words were cold and clipped, and the easy banter fell away from the three young men. Bernie licked his lips, the tip of his tongue darting out, snakelike.

"What did you say to me?"

"I told you to back away from the table."

"Mister, you don't think you can make words like that stick, do you?"

"I reckon I can."

"I don't know why I'm wastin' my time explainin'

things to a dried-up old bastard like you. Maybe I'm just an all-around nice guy. But maybe someone ought to tell you that when you're sittin' down and I'm standin' up, there's no way you can get a gun out faster'n me. Now, you goin' to back up them words? Or you goin' to eat 'em?"

"I reckon I'll back 'em up," Will said. During the entire confrontation, one of his hands had been under the table. Now he brought it above the table and everyone gasped, because he was holding a Colt .44. Will moved his lips into what could be called a smile, though the smile didn't quite reach the cold glint of his steel-blue eyes. "Looks like I did get it out faster, doesn't it? Now, you can try me, or you can go on about your business and leave us to ours."

The expression on the young cowboy's face changed from one of cockiness to fear. He put both hands up and started backing away.

"Listen, listen, mister," he said. "I didn't mean nothin' by all this. I was just funnin', that's all. You boys go on now and enjoy your game."

"We intend to," Will said.

The three cowboys walked away from the table.

Doc laughed. "Mister, if you won every hand for the rest of the night it would be worth it," he said. "I've been wanting to see somebody stand up to those boys."

Chapter Fourteen

The three cowboys stood drinking at the bar. They were considerably more subdued than they had been when they first came in. Bernie was drinking hard, tossing one whiskey down after another, while Jake and Sam tried to calm him down. Finally, Jake and Sam gave up and left Bernie to brood, while they walked over to a table occupied by Suzie and Smokey.

Although Gid had paid Suzie to drink with Smokey, it wasn't something she minded doing. She, like all the girls in the Redeye, liked Smokey. Nobody knew exactly how old he was, but it was said that he could remember the Alamo. It wasn't all that difficult for him to remember it....his father was one of the brave men who had died defending it.

"Hello, Suzie," Jake said.

Suzie looked at him, then turned back to talk to

Smokey.

"Hey, Jake, what do you think? It looks like Suzie don't love you no more," Sam suggested.

"Yeah? Well, we'll see about that," Jake retorted. "Look here, you old fart," he said to Smokey. "If you ain't goin' to take Suzie up to her room for a little fun, then quit chewin' her ears off and let someone do it who's still young enough to get the job done."

Smokey turned in his chair and looked up at Jake. "You go ahead, sonny," he said. "Take her upstairs. I'll still be here when she's finished."

"Go ahead, Jake. You got his permission," Sam teased.

"Yeah, well I don't need the son of a bitch's permission," Jake replied. He reached down to grab Suzie's arm, and she had to stand quickly to keep him from pulling her to her feet. "Tell you what, Smokey. Why don't you go back over there and have a drink with Bernie? This here ain't goin' to take very long."

Smokey chuckled. "No," he said. "I don't reckon it will."

"What's that s'posed to mean?" Jake growled.

"Why, it don't mean nothin', Jake," Smokey said. "I was just makin' conversation, that's all."

Jake laughed a high-pitched laugh. "Yeah, well, seem's that's 'bout all you're good for," he said. Tugging roughly on Suzie's arm, he pulled her over to the stairs, then started pushing her up to the second floor.

"I feel sorry for the girl," Dudley said.

Doc looked up. "Yeah, well, don't worry about Suzie. She's had plenty of experience handling people like that."

Though Will said nothing, he tended to agree with Doc. He didn't like to see any woman, even a soiled dove, mistreated, but it had been his observation over the years that women like Suzie were pretty good at protecting themselves.

Will lost this hand, then pushed away from the table.

"I appreciate the game, gentlemen," he said. "But I think I'll just have a drink or two, then call it a night. Thanks for letting me sit in."

"We enjoyed your company, mister. New blood's always welcome if it's friendly," Doc said. "What about it, Dudley? Another deal?"

"Not for me, thanks," Dudley replied. "I think I'll call it a night too."

"Me too," Neil added. "We may as well break up the game now or Bernie will be over here again wantin' to play."

"Yeah, I'll go along with that," Al said.

"You fellas can quit if you want to, but I'd like to get the winning edge back," Doc said. "There are a couple of other games going on now. I think I'll see if I can join one of them."

ROBERT VAUGHAN

Will said good-bye to his new friends, then walked over to the bar and ordered a drink. He had taken only one sip when the bat-wing doors swung open and a man wearing a badge stepped into the saloon.

"It's Sheriff Lacy," someone said.

"Smoke's goin' to fly now, fellas," another put in. "He done give them three boys the word not to come back to town 'till they paid off the damages."

"Bernie Yates," Sheriff Lacy called.

"Hello, Lacy. What got you away from your coffee and your nice cushioned chair?"

"I smelled a stink in the air and I figured you was over here," Sheriff Lacy replied. "Did you bring a hundred dollars to cover the damages you caused the other night?"

"I told you I wasn't goin' to pay for them damages," Bernie said without turning around.

"Then I reckon you'll be spendin' some time in jail."

Bernie and Sam both turned toward the sheriff. Bernie smiled evilly at him.

"I don't reckon I'd care to do that, Lacy," Bernie said. "You see, I'm pretty much what you'd call an outdoors man. Gettin' locked up in a jail ain't for me."

Sheriff Lacy held out his hand. "Give me your gun, Bernie," he said. "You too, Sam."

Bernie shook his head, the evil smile still pasted across his mouth.

"You want our guns, sheriff, you're goin' to have to take 'em away from us. That is, if you think you're able to do it."

At Bernie's challenging words there was a sudden frenzied movement as people in the line of fire hurried to get out of the way. Only Bernie and Sam remained at the bar. Even Will moved to the far end to be out of the way of any wild shot, should shooting break out.

"It doesn't have to be this way, boys," the sheriff said. "A few broken windows and chairs? It hardly seems worth dyin' over."

"That all depends on who's goin' to be doin' the dyin'," Bernie said, moving his hand in position just over the handle of his pistol. "You see, the way I'm figurin' is, it ain't goin' to be me."

Will was a little surprised by Bernie's bravado. He had already proven himself to be a braggart and a loud-mouth, but when it came right down to it, braggarts and loudmouths usually caved in to calm courage. And this sheriff had already impressed Will with the fact that he was a no-nonsense, courageous man. What, then, was giving Bernie his edge?

Will sensed, more than saw or heard, the movement at the top of the stairs. When he looked up, he saw Jake aiming at the sheriff. So, this was why Bernie was so confident. He knew that Jake was upstairs with the drop on the sheriff, while the sheriff had no idea of the additional threat.

Ordinarily, Will would never interfere in another man's fight. There were many reasons why he stayed out of them. Most of the time people resented interference, even if it had been undertaken with the best of intentions. Other times he just didn't know which side to back. This time, however, he had no problem in deciding. He had met the three cowboys and already disliked them enough to be partial to anyone who might be opposed to them. As it turned out, that was all the justification he needed to give the warning.

"Sheriff, there's a man on the landing with the drop on you," Will warned loudly.

Angry that his ambush plans were spoiled by Will's yell, Jake turned his gun on Will.

"You son of a bitch!" he shouted, pulling the trigger even as he yelled.

Will jumped to one side, pulling his pistol and shooting almost as quickly as Jake. The slug that Jake fired from the balcony missed Will and slammed into the glass mirror behind the bar. The mirror shattered and fell, leaving only a few jagged shards hanging in place to reflect, in distorted images, the scene playing before it.

Jake didn't get away a second shot because Will had fired right on top of him, and Will's bullet found its mark.

Jake dropped his pistol and grabbed his throat, then stood there, clutching his neck, as blood oozed between his fingers. Then his eyes rolled up into his head, and he twisted and fell, sliding head first down the stairs and following his clattering pistol all the way to the bottom. He lay motionless on the lowest step, his open but sightless eyes staring vacantly at the ceiling.

Will was still watching Jake slide down the stairs when he heard the roar of two more Colts. Though it seemed to him that time had stilled, thus causing a great separation between his and Jake's shots, and the next two shots, the truth was that the battle between Bernie and the sheriff had taken place almost simultaneously with his own fight.

Bernie had fired at the sheriff first, but his shot was badly placed. All it did was put a hole in the sheriff's hat. The sheriff's shot hit Bernie in the forehead and Bernie slid down to the floor in the sitting position, his body held up by the bar, his hands lying on the floor to each side of him. Like Jake, Bernie had been killed instantly.

"No, no, don't shoot! Don't shoot!" Sam shouted, holding his hands up in the air. "I ain't in this fight! I ain't in this fight!"

"Shuck your belt," the sheriff ordered.

"I'm doin' it, I'm doin' it," Sam said, using his left hand to unfasten his belt buckle. The gun belt dropped to the floor with a clatter.

The sheriff looked at Sam for a long moment, and Will thought he was going to shoot him anyway. Finally he sighed, and made a waving motion with his pistol.

"Get out of here, Sam," the sheriff said. "Just thank God you got out of here alive. Leave town and don't ever come back."

"But Bernie and Jake," Sam said, looking at two dead bodies with a sweep of his eyes.

"We'll take care of the dead," the sheriff promised. "Now, if you don't want to wind up in jail for a very long time ... get out of here."

"I'm goin', I'm goin'," Sam said, starting for the door.

The sheriff looked toward Will, then put his pistol away. Will did the same.

"I owe you my thanks, mister," he said.

"Yeah, well, I didn't plan to get involved," Will said. "But he didn't leave me much choice."

The sheriff looked at Will, then up toward the top of the stairs where Jake had been standing. He saw someone there holding a gun, and his hand dipped toward his own pistol.

"No, sheriff!" Will called. "It's all right! He's my brother!"

The sheriff nodded, then relaxed.

"That's a pretty good shot, you made, mister," the

sheriff said to Will. "I'd say it was better'n sixty feet. Would you agree?"

"That's as good a guess as any," Al said.

"It's seventy-five feet if it's an inch," Doc insisted.

The sheriff had gone over to Jake and was now examining the cowboy's wound. He didn't need to examine Bernie. With a hole in his forehead, his eyes wide open and opaque, and in the sitting position, leaning back against the bar, Bernie was very obviously dead.

"Seventy-five feet," Doc added, "and the bullet caught old Jake-boy here, right in the windpipe. Yes, sir, I'd say that was one hell of a shot."

The sheriff studied Will for a moment, then he looked up at Gid. "Say, I know you boys, don't I?"

"I don't believe we've had the pleasure," Will replied.

"You're right, we've never met in person," the sheriff agreed. He shook his finger slightly as he pointed it at Will. "But there's no need for us to have met for me to know who you are. You and your brother are the Crocketts. I've had paper on both of you."

Will shook his head. "Far as I know, Sheriff, we aren't wanted out here.

"This was when I was sheriffin' back in Kansas."

"You're from Kansas?"

"That's right," the sheriff said.

"I reckon that sort of makes us natural enemies,"

Will said.

Sheriff Lacy rubbed his chin for a moment, then shook his head. "Well, if we ever was enemies, we ain't no more," he said. "What you just done squares things in my book."

"Glad to hear it," Will said.

"What you two doin' here?" the sheriff asked.

"We're looking for someone."

"These fellas?"

Will looked over at the two bodies. By now, they had been picked up and laid out side by side on one of the longer tables. "No," he said. "They just happened to get in the way."

"Who are you after?"

"I think I can tell you that," Doc volunteered.

"Oh? And who would that be?" the sheriff asked.

"Unless I missed my guess, he's after Charley Kellett," Doc suggested to the sheriff. Then he looked directly at Will. "That was pretty slick of you, Will, to get into a card game with us just so you could get information," he added.

"I've learned that sometimes it's better to take the long way around," Will explained.

"I guess that's right most of the time," Doc replied. "But the truth is, there isn't a man here who doesn't want to see Charley Kellett get his due. In case you missed what we were saying awhile ago, a fire down in Rattlesnake Canyon this time of year is awfully curious."

Lacy chuckled. "Doc, do you know you're givin' away information that's worth fifteen-hundred dollars?"

"Fifteen-hundred-dollars? How do you figure?" Doc asked.

"There's five-hundred dollars reward money out on Charley Kellett, Donnie Hamilton, Perry Hoyt, and Jasper Moody," he said.

"Not Donnie Hamilton," Will said.

"Yeah, him too," the sheriff insisted. "He's worth as much as either one of the other fellas."

"Not anymore. Hamilton is dead," Will said, matter-of-factly.

"Dead? What happened to him?"

"I killed him," Gid said, speaking for the first time.

"That would explain it then," the sheriff said.

"Explain what?"

"Why there was only two men seen in the bank holdup over at Crawford. Witnesses swear that the only ones they saw were Kellett and Moody. Maybe that's because that's all there were. But that only takes care of Donnie Hamilton. It leaves a fella to wonderin' where Perry Hoyt might be."

"They split up when we were tracking them," Will said. "Hamilton and one man, who I am now sure was

Perry Hoyt, went one way. Kellett and Moody went another. Unfortunately, we went after the wrong pair. We caught up with Hamilton. I wanted Kellett."

"Why him, anymore than the others? They're all worth the same amount of money," the sheriff said.

"Because Kellett is the one we want," Gid said.

The sheriff nodded. "You aren't in this for the money, are you?"

"Sheriff, we'd go after that son of a bitch if we had to pay the reward ourselves," Will said.

"Wait a minute," the sheriff said. "I think I see it now. You boys must've had a run-in with Kellett during the war."

"Not quite," Will replied.

"What do you mean, 'not quite'?"

"What my brother means is, if we had run into Kellett during the war, he would be dead by now."

"Yes," the sheriff said. "Well, as far as I'm concerned, whatever reason you have is your own business. Kellett is a murderer, and the quicker someone takes care of him, the better off everyone will be. So, if the knowledge that he may be poking around down in Rattlesnake Canyon is useful to you, then use it with my blessing."

"Thanks," Will said. "I reckon we'll be checking that place out."

Will and Gid weren't the only ones to hear the possible location of Kansas Charley Kellett. Sam Rhodes had been run out of the saloon a few minutes earlier by the sheriff, but he hadn't actually gone anywhere. Right now he was standing in the shadows by the bat-wing doors, just outside the saloon. With his back to the wall and a small, two-shot sleeve-gun cradled in his raised right hand, Sam planned to shoot the sheriff the moment he stepped outside.

However, as he listened, he began to have other plans. If Kellett was worth money to the Crocketts, how much money would they be worth to Kellett?

The player at the card table hadn't been the only one who saw the campfire last night. Sam, Jake, and Bernie had seen it too. And not only did Sam know where it was, he knew a shorter way to get there. If he could get to Kellett before the Crocketts and provide him with information as to when and where the two brothers would come for him, Kellett might be very grateful. He might even let him join up with him.

Chapter Fifteen

Sam was pretty deep into the canyon at the mouth of Cottonwood Draw. Though there were literally dozens of draws and gullies in the canyon that would offer shelter, Cottonwood Draw was the only one that offered a way back out. If Kellett knew that as well, then this is where he would be.

Sam stopped just outside the mouth of the draw, then climbed up onto a protruding finger and looked over into it. It was too dark to see anything, so he decided to wait until dawn. He was alone, and he didn't know how many men might be with Kellett. He had no desire to stumble into the camp in the middle of the night. That would be a good way to get himself killed.

When Sam looked to the East he could see a faint streak of pearl-gray. It wouldn't be much longer, until it would be light enough for him to approach. He could afford to wait it out. If they would listen to him and believe him, they would still have time to prepare an ambush for the Crocketts.

Sam pulled a strip of jerky from his saddlebag, chewed off a piece, then wrapped what remained in the soiled and greasy waxed paper he kept it in. He chewed it for several minutes and it seemed to get bigger and bigger in his mouth. He wanted to spit it out, but he figured he would need the sustenance, so he continued to work at it. He finally managed to get the last bit down, then he followed that with a swallow of water. He wished it was coffee, but he knew that starting a fire would be foolish, perhaps even fatal.

The night finally lifted, illuminating the canyon floor in a soft, coral light, though lingering shadows still hung in the corners and edges of the deeper draws. Sam climbed up to the top of the protruding finger and looked down into Cottonwood Draw once more. This time he saw the camp, but he was surprised to see that there was only one person there. He thought there was supposed to be at least two of them, maybe three. Where were the others?"

"Oh, you clever bastards," he said quietly. "You're keeping two men on watch while one sleeps. That way nobody can sneak in on you."

He wondered, though, why they had not yet come

153

in. He also wondered why the lone man in camp had not built a fire for their morning coffee. Maybe they were being cautious. Why weren't they cautious the other night? Every nighthawk within twenty miles had seen the fire then.

Sam chuckled to himself as he thought of an old saying. He said it aloud.

"You boys have done shut the barn door after the horse is gone," he said.

Sam stood up, brushed his hands together, then started walking down the other side of the little hill, leading his horse into the campsite.

"Hello the camp!" he called, holding his arm out so that anyone watching could clearly see that he wasn't carrying a weapon. "Hello the camp! I'm a friend!"

No lookouts came in, nor did they even make their presence known.

"Mr. Kellett?" Sam called. "Charley Kellett? My name is Sam Rhodes. I've come to join you, if I may."

Still no answer, nor movement. Even the one person in the camp was still.

"Listen, I want to warn you. Them Crockett brothers is on their way. Someone give 'em the information that you was out here. It wasn't me," he added. "I swear, it wasn't me. I just overheard, which is how come I'm here. What you shouldn't of done is to build a fire at night.

Them things can be seen for a long, long ways."

Sam was beginning to get a little disconcerted when no one answered.

"Mister, are you asleep? You can't be asleep. Hell, I done made more noise than a herd of cows comin' into this camp." By now Sam was right over the supine figure, and he squatted down to touch him on the shoulder. "What's the matter with you?"

The man on the ground suddenly rolled over. Sam saw a flash of movement, then felt the barrel of the man's pistol under his chin. He heard the hammer being cocked.

"Who are you?" the man asked.

"Sam Rhodes, Sam Rhodes," Sam said in fright, backing away so quickly that he fell on his back. "Don't shoot! Don't shoot!"

The man sat up, though it seemed to be with some effort. He held his gun leveled toward Sam. "What are you doing here?" he asked.

"I came to warn you and the others about the Crockett Brothers."

The man with the gun laughed, then he winced with pain and put his hand down to his hip. That was when Sam saw that the man's right leg was caked with dried blood.

"You're hurt?" he asked.

"Yeah. Some kid shot me with a .22." He laughed

again, a dry, brittle laugh. "Can you believe that? Jasper Moody getting' shot by a kid? With a .22? You got any water?"

"I got a canteen."

"Give me some water."

"I ain't got that much, but..."

"I said give me some water!" Moody cocked his pistol.

"Sure thing, mister. Didn't say I wasn't goin' to give you none," Sam said, reaching for his canteen. He tossed it to Moody, and Moody pulled the cork, then began drinking thirstily.

"You're Jasper Moody?"

"Yeah, that's me." Moody said, taking the canteen down and squinting up at Sam. "Who'd you say you was again?"

"My name is Sam, Mr. Moody. Sam Rhodes."

"What are you doin' out here, Sam?"

"Like I told you, I came to warn you fellas about the Crocketts."

"Why would you do that?"

"Well, for one thing, I don't like the sons of bitches very much," Sam said. "One of 'em killed a friend of mine yesterday. And for another, I thought maybe you and Mr. Kellett would let me join up with you."

Moody laughed again, another dry, brittle, laugh.

"You want to ride the outlaw trail do you, Sam?" he asked.

"Yes."

"You're bold and brave to want to join that gallant band of brothers whose home is the wind and whose destiny is danger?"

"What?"

Moody laughed heartily. "I got that from one of those dime novels some fool wrote about Charley Kellett. Kellett carries them with him, you know, and if he finds somebody who hasn't heard of him, he shows them the books."

"I never knew they wrote no books about Charley Kellett."

"You've never heard of Kansas Charley?"

"Sure, I've heard of 'im," Sam said. "I just never knew anyone had wrote any books about him."

Moody laughed again. "Charley won't like that," he said. "He sets a great store by them dime novels."

Sam looked around nervously.

"Where is he?" he asked. "I thought you two was together."

"Let's see. Where would ol' Charley be by now?" Moody asked. "By now I reckon he's watching the whores dance down in Black Rock."

"Black Rock? That's a hundred miles south of here,

near to the border."

"That's the general idea," Moody replied.

"But, what are you doin' here?" Sam looked around the campsite. "Where's your horse?"

"You noticed that, did you? My horse is gone. He took it with him, along with my share of the money from the bank job in Crawford and my water and food."

"Why did he leave you here like this?"

"I guess he thought I'd slow 'im down," Moody said. "Thanks for the water." He handed the canteen back to Sam.

"Sure," Sam said. As he was hooking the canteen back on the saddle, he saw a plume of dust in the distance, glowing brightly in the early morning sun.

"Someone's coming," he said.

"The Crocketts?"

"It has to be," Sam replied.

"You got a rifle?" Moody asked.

"Yeah, I got a rifle."

"Tell you what you do. You tie your horse here, then you take your rifle and go over there, in those rocks and wait. I'll be the bait, you see. And when the Crocketts come into the camp, you'll have a perfect bead on 'em."

"Yeah," Sam said. "Yeah, that's a good idea."

"Leave me your pistol," Moody said.

"What?"

"Leave me your pistol."

"What do you want with my pistol?"

"That's a .37, ain't it?"

"Yes."

"Mine's a .44. I don't have no bullets, and what you got won't fit mine."

"You don't have no shells at all?"

"None," Moody replied. He thought of the empty, metal click, last night, when in despair he had put the pistol to his temple and pulled the trigger. "I reckon Charley thought I wouldn't have no need for 'em out here. When he left, he took everything, even the shells that was already loaded into my gun."

"No bullets at all, huh?" Sam smiled when he got the idea. "Well, I'll be damned."

Will and Gid stopped when they heard the shot, flat and low in the distance.

"Did you hear that?" Gid asked.

"Yeah, I heard it."

"They couldn't be shooting at us. We're too far away. So the question is, why did they shoot in the first place? They're just giving their position away."

"Could be that they know we're here and they're just lettin' us know they know," Will suggested.

"Maybe," Gid agreed.

"Well, come on, let's see this thing through."

As the brothers moved up the canyon floor, they stayed close to the wall, taking advantage of the rocks and protrusions, passing through apertures when possible, rather than going around or over the long fingers.

They moved cautiously to the top of a long promontory, then looked over to the other side. They saw a hobbled, saddled horse and Jasper Moody sitting nearby, holding a coffee cup and staring into the remains of a fire.

"There's one of them," Gid said. He started to move, but Will reached out and took his brother by the arm.

"Wait a minute, little brother," he said. "There's something wrong here."

"Yeah," Gid said, pulling back. "I see what you mean. It's kind of peculiar the way he's just sitting there. He hasn't taken a drink of his coffee, moved or even twitched."

"If that's coffee, where did it come from?" Will asked. "There's no pot anywhere, no smell of coffee in the air."

"And not the tiniest wisp of smoke from that fire," Gid added.

"Gid, I've got a gut instinct that Moody is dead," Will said. "That was what the shot was."

"You think Kellett killed him?"

"Yeah. They said the kid who was killed in Crawford hit one of the robbers. I figure he was slowing Kellett

JUDGEMENT DAY

down, so Kellett shot him, then left him here as a decoy."

"Wouldn't be the first time the bastard has turned on one of his own," Gid agreed.

The two men holstered their pistols, then started down into the camp.

Suddenly Will got an uneasy feeling. He could see one saddle on the ground beside the propped-up body of Jasper Moody, and another on the horse.

"Gid, something's wrong!" Will shouted. "There's one saddle too many here!"

At that moment a rifle cracked, and the bullet whistled by, taking off Will's hat and fluffing his hair. Both Will and Gid leaped down from their horses and dived to the ground. They began wriggling on their bellies toward a small rock outcropping, reaching it just as a second shot came so close that Will could hear the air pop as the bullet sped by.

When the brothers made it to the rocks, they raised up slowly and looked toward the sound of the shot. Will didn't see anyone, but he did see a little puff of white smoke drifting slowly to the East. He pointed to the smoke, then to Gid, and Gid nodded.

The wind was out of the West, which meant that the shooter had to be somewhat west of the smoke. Will shifted his eyes in that direction, then saw the crown of a hat, rising slowly above the rocks. He waited until he thought enough of the hat was visible to provide a target, then he shot. The hat went sailing away.

"You son of a bitch! You put a hole in my hat!"

"I meant to put a hole in your head," Will replied. He was puzzled by the voice. It wasn't Charley Kellett or Perry Hoyt. Who was it?

The ambusher fired again. The bullet hit the rock right in front of Will, kicking up tiny pieces of rock and shreds of hot lead into his face before it whined away behind him. Will turned around and slid down into the ground, brushing the hot lead from his cheeks.

"Did I hit you?" the man called.

"Close, but no cigar," Will replied. "Who the hell are you?"

The man laughed. "You don't recognize me?" he asked. "All I can say is, you sure got yourself one hell of a short memory."

Will remembered now ... not the name, but the voice.

"He was in the saloon last night," Gid said. "He was with the two who got themselves killed."

"That's right. The name's Sam Rhodes, in case you forgot."

"Sam Rhodes," Will said. "I'll try to remember that."

"You won't have to remember it too long," Sam said. He fired again, coming incredibly close. Will realized then that Sam Rhodes wasn't just another wild cowboy with a gun. He was very good with the rifle.

"I'll say this for you, Sam Rhodes. You handle that rifle pretty well."

"Yeah," Sam said. "Back in the saloon, last night, there wasn't no way I was goin' to go up against you or the sheriff with a pistol. But with a rifle, now, that's a different story. I've won the Fourth July rifle-shooting contest for the last five years running."

"That's pretty good," Will said.

"Yeah," Sam replied. "Good enough I figure to go into a new business."

"Ridin' the outlaw trail's not that smart a move," Gid said.

"Outlaw trail? No way. I'm goin' over to the other side of the law. I aim to take Moody in and collect on him, then I'm going after Kellett."

"You're going to be a bounty hunter?" Will asked.

"That's right," Sam replied. "I come out here to join up with 'em, only I found Moody here, all alone. The others had gone on to Black Rock without him. Me and Moody got to talkin', and the next thing you know, I find out he's worth five hundred dollars. He wasn't lyin' to me, was he? He is worth five hundred dollars?"

"He wasn't lying," Will answered.

"Five hundred dollars. What do you know about that? That's a lot of money," Sam said. "So I got to thinkin' about it. Why should I join up with these fellas and get a price on my head, when I could just kill 'em, 'n get the reward myself? So, I killed the son of a bitch."

"Seems like the reasonable thing to do," Will replied. To Gid, Will whispered, "Keep him talking."

During the entire conversation Will had been slipping out of his boots, pants, and shirt. Now he put them on the ground behind where he had taken cover, arranging them so that, at a casual glance from a distance, it would look as if he were there. Then, barefooted and half-naked, he put the blade of his knife between his teeth and slipped away.

"Sam, can I ask you a question?" Gid called, as he watched his brother leave.

"Go ahead."

"If you really are going into the bounty-hunting business, why are you trying to kill us. We don't have any money on our heads."

"Well, let's look at it this way," Sam replied. "You boys are going after Kellett. I heard you say so last night. If you find him before I do ... you'll get the reward. I don't aim to let that happen."

"So, you're willing to kill us just to get us out of the way?" Gid asked.

"That's true,' Sam said. Almost instantly after saying the words, Sam fired. Gid was just changing positions at that moment in order to relieve his back. The bullet from Sam's rifle seared his cheek as it took out a chunk of flesh. Blood began running down the side of Gid's face. If he had not moved at that exact moment, he would be dead.

"Did I get you?" Sam called.

"Hate to disappoint you," Gid called back. "But you missed me by a mile." Even as he was telling the lie, he was holding his handkerchief to his face to stop the bleeding.

After having gone some thirty yards, Will found himself in a narrow, twisting fissure that worked its way down the side of the canyon, passing fairly close to where Sam had taken cover.

Will stepped into the fissure and, putting his bare feet and hands on either side, began climbing.

Sam fired again and his bullet nicked the heel of Will's boot, knocking it back behind the rock.

"Ha!" Sam shouted. "I'll just reckon that stung a mite, didn't it? That'll learn you to keep your foot out where I can see it."

Will continued to climb until he reached a ledge. Once there, he left the fissure and crawled out onto it. Then, on his stomach, he wriggled over to the edge and looked down. Sam was no more than twenty yards below him. Sam was peering around the side of a rock, looking toward the place where he had last seen Will and Gid.

"Hey, Crocketts! How come you ain't shootin' back?"

Sam called. "You boys ain't out of shells are you? Course, if you was, I don't reckon you'd tell me. I mean, Jasper Moody told me an' look what it got 'im. He told me he was out of bullets and I shot him. Like you said, it seemed like the reasonable thing to do."

Sam fired again.

"If you keep shooting at rocks, you're going to run out of bullets yourself," Will said easily.

Startled, Sam turned around. The expression in his face reflected the shock of seeing Will, not only in a place totally different from where Sam thought he was, but also because Will was naked, except for a pair of underbriefs.

"What the hell?" Sam shouted, swinging his rifle around, while, at the same time, jacking in a new round.

Sam got the lever down, but he never pulled it back up. Will's right arm whipped forward and the knife flashed once in the sun as it sped across the distance between the two men. It buried itself to the hilt in Sam's chest, penetrating his heart and killing him even before he could fully realize what was happening to him.

Chapter Sixteen

Black Rock was on the American side of the border, but there were far more Mexicans than Americans who lived there. The land was arid and too poor for farming or ranching, though many tried, and a few even managed to eke out a meager existence. There were some who searched for gold or silver, and though little of those commodities were found, enough nuggets turned up to hold out tantalizing prospects. Thus the hunt continued.

Despite the bleakness of its agricultural and mining prospects, Black Rock was, nevertheless, a bustling town. It saw a surprising amount of money flow through its half-dozen saloons, whorehouses, gaming establishments, cafes, and hotels. Outlaws fleeing south often used Black Rock for one last American fling. And since many of those same outlaws were fleeing from bank robberies or other sources of ill-gotten gains, money was in abundance. On the other hand, Mexicans just arriving in America would often spend their life savings in one afternoon, too ignorant of the exchange system to know they were being cheated.

Black Rock had a sheriff and two deputies. One wall in the sheriff's office was decorated with wanted posters from both sides of the border. However, neither Sheriff Eaton nor his deputies had ever made any attempt to apprehend any of the men on the wanted posters. If they had tried, they would have incurred the immediate wrath of the town's business community, for outlaws on the run were the main source of income. As a result, a man who had a price on his head in Texas, Colorado, Wyoming, or some such place was just as welcome in Black Rock as any other traveler.

The outlaws were very aware of Sheriff Eaton's policy toward wanted men, so they were always on their best behavior in his town and around him. In fact, some of them even became friends with him and the sheriff's "rogues' gallery" became somewhat well known throughout the Southwest for a most unique reason. Almost three-quarters of the wanted posters on the wall in the sheriff's office were autographed by the very outlaw whose face graced the dodger.

Kellett was very familiar with Black Rock, having been there many times before. But he wasn't the only one

168

who knew about the town. Perry Hoyt knew about it as well, and he was waiting in a little grove of cottonwood trees about a quarter of a mile out of town. The sun had already set when Hoyt saw Kellett riding by.

"Charley?" Hoyt called to him from the shadows.

"Hoyt!" Kellett answered in surprise. "What are you doin' here?"

Hoyt mounted, then rode out into the road to join Kellett. "I figured if you was still alive, you'd wind up here," Hoyt answered. "So, I just waited."

"Yeah, well, as you can see, I'm still alive."

"Where's Moody?" Hoyt asked.

"He didn't make it," Kellett replied.

"What happened?"

"Moody and me ... we tried to hold up a bank in Crawford. The whole damn town was layin' for us. We had to shoot our way out of the bank. Moody got hit as we were ridin' out. He died on the trail a couple of days later. Wasn't nothin' I could do for him. What about Hamilton?"

"Me 'n him split up," Hoyt said. "I figured maybe we'd meet up here, but I ain't seen hide nor hair of him since we took out on our own. I figure the Crocketts musta got 'im."

"Prob'ly so," Kellett agreed.

"You say you an' Moody held up a bank?"

"Yeah."

"Did you get 'ny money?"

Kellett thought of the nearly two-hundred dollars he had in his saddlebag. "We got about fifty dollars," he lied. "What about you? You got any money?"

"No more'n a couple bucks," Hoyt answered.

Kellett stuck his hand down in his pocket, then pulled out twenty dollars. "Here," he said.

"What's this?"

"Moody's share. He won't be needin' it."

Hoyt was surprised. "Thanks, Charley."

"Come on, let's ride into town and get a drink," Kellett offered.

"You been in this town before?" Hoyt asked.

"Yeah, lots of times," Kellett replied.

"What about the sheriff?"

"Don't worry none about the sheriff. All you gotta do when we get there is keep your nose clean," Kellett told him. "And don't get in any fights."

"You don't need to worry about that. I plan to stay outta trouble."

"That's good."

"I hope they got somethin' to eat in this town, though. I'm getting' hungry for somethin' more'n jerky and thirsty for somethin' more'n trail water."

"Well, you've come to the right place," Kellett said. "Black Rock is known for good food and good whiskey."

170

"I could also use me a woman."

Kellett chuckled. "Oh, yeah, Black Rock is known for its whores, too."

"Food, liquor, and whores," Hoyt repeated. "And I got me twenty dollars. What else would a man need?"

"Maybe more money," Kellett suggested. "Twenty dollars ain't goin' to go very far here. The problem with this town is, don't nobody hardly come here, 'cept if they're wanted. That means the town's got us by the balls, and they know it. Everything here costs two or three times more'n it costs anywhere else."

"Hell, I don't care how much things cost. It's not like I'm plannin' on buyin' me a shirt and a pair of boots."

"It ain't just the merchants," Kellett explained. "Anywhere else in the country a man can get him a whore to share his bed for two dollars. Here, they want five dollars."

"Would them whores be Mexican or American?" Hoyt asked.

"Both, I reckon. Why, does it matter?"

Hoyt chuckled. "Long as they spread their legs, it don't matter to me whether they be Americans or Mex."

Black Rock was dark except for the patches of light that spilled out into the street from the windows and doors of the cantinas. The town was noisy, as several guitars competed with each other for attention. A few people were singing, and in the back of one of the cantinas, a trumpet ran through several high trills. Laughter and loud voices filled the night air, and occasionally a gunshot would ring out, though the people knew instinctively that the gunshots were in boisterous fun and nothing more.

"Hey, fellas," a woman called down to them from an upstairs balcony as they rode by. She was leaning over the balcony banister, wearing nothing but an undergarment, and it was cut low enough to expose the tops of enormous breasts. But her breasts were large because she was large. "Hey, fellas, why don't you come on up here?" she invited. "I don't charge as much as any of the other girls."

With her red hair, pasty-white complexion, and flat, twangy accent, she was definitely American.

"You want to give her a try?" Kellett asked.

Hoyt looked up at the woman, then laughed. "No, I don't think so," he said. He rubbed his crotch. "You know, I think I'll get me a little black-eyed Mexican girl. I like them girls. Course, you got to be careful you don't get a in'jun. Sometimes it's hard to tell the difference. I got me a woman one time back in Arizona Territory ... thought she was Mexican but she turned out to be in'jun. The only thing that pissed me off is she charged as much as a Mexican whore, and I don't think you ought to pay as much for a in'jun as you do a Mex. Course, you ought not to have to pay for any woman. Say, Kellett, you ever had a woman you didn't have to pay for?"

"Yeah," Kellett said.

"When? Where?"

Kellett recalled the young Patton girl he and Alvarado had raped. She was young, almost too young, but when they took her clothes off, he saw that she was beginning to shape up like a woman. He rubbed himself now, as he thought about it.

To be as young as she was, she had fought like a tiger. He finally had to knock her out so that, when he and Alvarado took her, she was as still as if she were dead.

Alvarado complained a little. He said he wanted more life in the women he had, but Kellett reminded him that any woman, even a woman who wasn't moving, was better than no woman at all.

When they were both finished with her, Kellett tried to bring her to, but she wouldn't wake up. He started jabbing her with his knife. He hadn't really intended for what happened next to happen. But for some reason he couldn't explain ... seeing her dark, red blood stream across her milky-white, naked skin did something to him. Before he realized what he was doing, he was stabbing her, over and over again.

"You didn't have to kill her," Alvarado said. "If you'd'a kept her alive, we could'a had some more fun with her."

Kellett looked down at the young Patton girl's

ROBERT VAUGHAN

pubescent body and at the trails of blood, drying now on her white skin.

"Ah, she was half-dead anyway," he finally said. He knelt beside her, then grabbed one of her small breasts and began to carve.

"What the hell are you a doin'?" Alvarado asked.

"I'm getting' me a souvenir," Kellett said.

Kellett hacked off the girl's breast and took it with him. Then, after he got away from the Crocketts in the night shootout at the monastery, he scraped the flesh out, dried the skin, and made it into a tobacco pouch. He had never actually used it as a tobacco pouch, though he did carry it with him.

"I've got her tit," he added matter of factly.

"You've got what?" Hoyt asked, surprised by Kellett's comment.

"You asked if I ever had me a woman I didn't pay for. I answered, yes, I did," Kellett said. "And I've got her tit."

"You've got her tit?"

"Yes. You want to see it?" He reached down into his pocket and pulled out a small, dry, leathery object and handed it over to Hoyt.

Hoyt, thinking it was a joke, took it from him. At first he was sure that it was leather, then he saw a little spongy protrusion and, curiously examined it more closely. Then suddenly he realized that the little piece of sponge was actually a nipple. When he realized that, he let out a little shout and threw it.

"Son of a bitch!" Hoyt shouted. "It really is a tit!"

"Damnit, what'd you throw it away for?" Kellett asked irritably. He got down from his horse and picked it up from the dirt, wiping it off before putting it back in his pocket.

"What the hell is the matter with you? You crazy? How can you carry somethin' like that around with you?" Hoyt asked.

Kellett laughed. "What are you gettin' so upset about?" Kellett asked. ' "This here tit come off a young, white-trash Secesh. Anyhow, where do you get off findin' fault with me? It ain't like you ain't never been a part of killin' a woman. You was there when we kilt the Doc's wife, and if you ever get caught, you are going to hang as high as me over that one."

"Maybe so, but we didn't cut off her tit," Hoyt said.

"She wouldn't of felt it, if we had cut it off," Kellett said. "Same as this girl. She didn't feel a thing. Come on, let's quit palavarin' and get to drinkin'."

The drinking establishment was much more Mexican in flavor than American, even to the point that entry was through a clacking curtain of beaded strings, rather than through the more American, bat-wing doors. Inside, the bar was noisy with conversation, half of it in

Spanish, half in English.

"Hello, Senor," a pretty, young Mexican girl said, coming up to Hoyt. "I am very thirsty and I do not want to drink alone. You will drink with me?"

Hoyt started to reach for her, then he saw the top of her full, creamy breast spilling out over her low-cut blouse. He thought of the little piece of leather he had handled just a moment earlier and his blood ran cold. He turned away from her.

"No," he said. "Go find someone else."

"What the hell's the matter with you?" Kellett asked, surprised by Hoyt's strange reaction. "I thought you said you wanted some good-lookin' Mexican gal."

"No ... not now, not yet," Hoyt replied, not wanting to explain to Kellett why he was feeling like he was.

"Well if you don't want her, I do," Kellett said. He put his arm around the girl. "Come on, honey. You want a drink, let's get a whole bottle and go upstairs."

Of the two men, Kellett was clearly the least attractive to the woman. In fact, there was something almost frightening about him. That was why she had made her initial overture to Hoyt. But he had refused, and she was in a business where she couldn't afford to be choosy. So she kept the disappointment hidden behind her eyes and pasted on a smile.

"All right," she said to Kellett. "If your friend does

not want me, then I will go with you." Teasingly, she put her hand in Kellett's hair and twisted a strand of it around her finger. "If you want me," she added, coquettishly.

"Honey, you come with me and I'll show you just how much I want you," Kellett said, grabbing her and walking over to the bar to buy a bottle.

Hoyt watched Kellett and the Mexican girl take their bottle up the stairs, then he, too, walked over to the bar.

"Can I get anything to eat here?" he asked.

"Frijoles. Tamales," the bartender answered.

"Anything American?"

"Eggs, Senor."

"Steak?"

The bartender nodded. "Si, steak too."

"Fix me a steak and some eggs," Hoyt said. "And let me have a pitcher of beer."

"Si, Senor Hoyt. Anything you want," the bartender replied.

Hoyt looked surprised. "You know who I am? You recognize me?"

"No, but Senor Kellett called you Hoyt. Is that not your name, Senor?"

The smile left Hoyt's face. For a fleeting moment there, he thought he had achieved a degree of fame. "Yeah," he said, somewhat crestfallen. "Yeah, that's my name."

Chapter Seventeen

Perry Hoyt took the pitcher of beer from the bartender and walked over to a corner, where he found an empty table. He sat down with his back to the wall and began drinking his beer. Then he reached into his back pocket and pulled out a rolled-up dime novel and laid it on the table.

He had bought the dime novel long before he actually met Kellett. He wouldn't admit it to anyone ... especially not to Kellett... but sometimes he secretly dreamed of the day someone would write a penny dreadful about him.

The pages were torn and the printing was getting dim from sweat, grime, and wear. The drawing on the cover was still discernible, however, and Hoyt studied it for a long time. It showed a man on a horse, fleeing before a posse. Hanging across the pommel of his saddle were two large bags, and if the reader couldn't figure out what the bags were, they were clearly marked by oversized dollar signs. A train was in the background. The door of the mail car was open and someone was standing in the opening, holding his fist over his head. A word-balloon from the mouth of the character said, "It's Kansas Charley! He has just robbed the express!"

There were several people leaning out of the open windows of the cars on the train, and all of them seemed to be armed and shooting at the fleeing robber. The robber, who according to the book was Kansas Charley Kellett, was holding the reins of his horse in his teeth while he was twisted around in the saddle, firing both guns at the pursuing posse, two of whom were in the process of falling from their saddles with mortal wounds inflicted by Kansas Charley's unerring pistol fire.

The cover left unexplained how a posse managed to arrive on the scene so quickly that the train Kansas Charley had just robbed was still sitting on the tracks. It also did not take into account the fact that, of all the crimes for which the real Charley Kellett was charged with, none of them involved robbing a train, which was in fact, much too dangerous an operation for Charley to ever consider.

The name of the novel was: Kansas Charley's Bold Midnight Robbery of the Denver Express, though the robbery depicted on the cover was very obviously taking place in daylight.

Hoyt began to read:

He came upon the train with both guns blazing and the reins of his horse held in his teeth. "Stand and deliver!" he shouted in a voice that was both heroic and frightening.

Hoyt wondered how anyone could even talk with the reins in his teeth, let alone sound off in a voice that was both heroic and frightening. And though he had never used the line "Stand and deliver," he was pretty sure Kellett, about whom this book was supposedly written, had never used it either. But it did have a good ring to it and he decided that in his very next holdup he would use it.

"It is Kansas Charley," the engineer shouted to his fireman. His voice was laced with fear and respect, for Kansas Charley was known throughout the West as the deadliest shot alive. It has been reliably reported that he can shoot the leg off a fly at fifty paces.

There was a shower of sparks and the squeal of steel wheels sliding upon steel rails as the frightened engineer brought his great iron steed to rest.

"Open the doors of the express car or feel the fury of hot lead!" Kansas Charley demanded.

Though the armed guards of the express car were filled with the greatest of trepidation, the ladies of the train, all of whom had hurried to the windows as a more oppor-

tune place from which to get a good look, were strangely devoid of fear. They seemed, instead, romantically smitten by the handsome young man who sat astride his horse, holding the brace of pistols leveled at the express car door.

A plate of steak and eggs was put on the table in front of Hoyt, but he was too absorbed in the story to bother to look up. He reached for the steak and picked it up in his hands.

"Hoyt, you really need to work on your table manners, haven't you ever heard of a knife and fork?"

Gasping, Hoyt looked up to see that the person who had just delivered his food was not the bartender but Gid Crockett. Gid had his pistol out. He waved the end of the barrel.

"Go ahead, take a bite," he said. "I never liked to disturb a man before he was finished eatin' his supper."

Hoyt held the piece of meat just in front of his mouth, staring, wide-eyed at his captor.

"Go ahead, eat," Gid said again.

Hoyt raised the steak to his mouth, then, suddenly he dropped it and made a mad grab for his pistol. But Gid was quicker and he brought his pistol down hard on Hoyt's head. Hoyt fell like a poleaxed steer.

"You shouldn't read that trash, Hoyt," Gid said quietly. "You'll get to believing it."

Gid bent down to pick up Hoyt's pistol. Then he dragged Hoyt's limp, unconscious form over to one of the supporting posts, where he propped him, putting one arm to either side of the post. Then he tied Hoyt's hands together with a short piece of rope.

The guitar music, laughter, and conversation had all come to a stop when Gid knocked out Hoyt. Most of the other patrons looked on in curiosity, making no comment until they saw Gid put on the handcuffs. (not handcuffs, restraints, maybe?)

"Hey, what the hell? You a lawman, mister? 'Cause if you are, you got no jurisdiction here," someone said.

Gid looked over at the speaker. "Who are you?" he asked.

"I'm the man that's goin' to teach you better than to come into Black Rock when you ain't wanted. Who the hell are you?"

"The name is Crockett. Gid Crockett," Gid said. He pointed to Will, who was standing just inside the door, with his pistol drawn. "That's my brother, Will."

The man who had issued the challenge, measured the look in the eyes of the two brothers and realized that he was about to make a big mistake. He began dissembling.

"Listen, you boys don't pay me no never mind," he said in a frightened, quivering voice. "You go on about your business ... do whatever it is you come to Black Rock to do. You won't get no guff from me."

"Well now, that's very nice of you," Gid replied. He walked back over to the table where Hoyt had been sitting. His untouched steak had fallen back onto his plate and Gid sat down and began eating it. He picked up the pitcher of beer and took several swallows before he set it back down. The rest of the saloon continued to watch him in silence.

"Play," Gid said to the guitarist.

"Si, Senor," the guitarist said, and he began a heavy chording.

Will chuckled at his brother's confiscation of the unexpected meal. Then he walked over to the bar.

"There were two of 'em," Will said, holding up two fingers and indicating Hoyt, with a nod of his head.

"Si, Senor."

"Where's the other one?"

The bartender didn't answer, but he did cut his eyes up.

"Thanks," Will replied.

Upstairs, in the girl's bedroom, Kellett had heard the saloon below grow strangely quiet. He stopped.

"Are you finished, Senor?" the girl asked.

"Shut up," Kellett hissed.

"*Que?*" the girl asked, surprised by Kellett's harsh command.

"I said shut up!" Kellett hissed again, putting his hand over her mouth. When he was sure she wouldn't speak again, he pulled his hand away. The girl took a long, gasping breath.

Kellett sat up and swung his legs over the side of the bed, then reached for his pistol. It was still deathly quiet below. "Don't you hear that?" Kellett asked.

"I hear nothing, Senor," the girl said in a quiet, whimpering voice.

"Yeah, that's just it," Kellett said. "Neither do I."

Still holding his pistol, Kellett began slipping back into his pants. He was already buttoning them up when the guitar music started again. Even this, however, was different. Before the music had been soft and melodious, a single-string melody weaving in and out of gentle chording. Now it was loud, syncopated, and invasive.

Kellett slipped into his boots and kept his eye on the doorknob. He just got them on when he saw the knob move ever so slightly.

Kellett began firing, punching a pattern of six bullets through the door in such a way that one of them was sure to be fatal for whoever was on the other side.

With an angry shout, Kellett rushed across the room and kicked open the door. He ran out onto the landing just outside the door.

Will had jiggled the doorknob then stepped to one side, no more than a second before the fusillade of bullets. He had stood with his back to the wall, watching the spray of splinters as the bullets came through. Then he had heard Kellett's loud, angry shout as the outlaw dashed across the room. When Kellett appeared on the landing Will had brought his pistol crashing into the back of Kellett's head. The blow, plus the momentum of Kellett's rush, carried him through the banister, causing him to crash, belly down, onto one of the tables in the room below.

By the time Will reached the bottom of the stairs, Sheriff Eaton was stepping through the beaded curtains of the front door. He saw all the patrons of the saloon standing to one side or the other, giving Gid a lot of room.

"What the hell is goin' on here?" the sheriff asked.

"We have a couple of prisoners for you, Sheriff," Gid said. He pointed to Hoyt. "The one tied to the post is Perry Hoyt. The other one is Kansas Charley Kellett."

The sheriff shook his head. "I got no call to hold them two fellas," he said. "They ain't done nothin' in my town."

"All we want you to do is to keep 'em overnight while we get a little sleep. They're both wanted men," Gid said. "My brother and I will be takin' 'em back with us in the morning, soon as we get a little rest."

"They may be wanted men where you come from,

185

mister," the sheriff said. "But they ain't wanted here, and I'm not puttin' 'em in my jail."

By now Hoyt was conscious, and hearing the sheriff's refusal to cooperate, began to heckle Gid and Will.

"What are you two boys going to do now?" he asked. "Seems to me like you're 'bout at the end of your rope." He giggled loudly.

"Don't worry about it, Hoyt," Will said. "The sheriff has just changed his mind. He is going to keep you two for us, after all."

"What the hell you talkin' about?" Sheriff Eaton asked angrily. "I ain't changed my mind."

Will's draw was as quick as the flick of a rattler's tongue. He raised his pistol and pointed it at Sheriff Eaton. "Sheriff, you can go down to the jailhouse as their jailer or their cell mate. The choice is yours."

"Suppose I don't like either choice?" the sheriff replied.

"There is a third choice," Will explained. "You can go out of here stretched out on that door." He cocked his pistol.

"I'm the sheriff. You wouldn't shoot me."

Will fired. His bullet clipped off a tiny piece of the sheriff's left earlobe, sending out a spray of blood. The sheriff, with a shout of pain and terror, slapped his hand to his ear. The wound was bleeding profusely and the blood began streaming through his fingers.

"You're ... you're crazy!" the sheriff said.

Will moved the pistol to aim at the sheriff's other ear. Quickly, he covered it up.

"This time I'll take off a couple of fingers, too," Will suggested.

"No! No! Wait!" the sheriff said, holding his bloody hands, palm out toward Will. "Don't shoot again. I'll put 'em up for you!"

Will smiled and lowered his gun.

"I thank you for your cooperation," he said "Come first light in the mornin' my brother and I will be by for them."

Chapter Eighteen

The next morning, a crowing rooster awakened Will just before first light. He sat up, stretched, pulled on his boots, then walked over to the chifforobe where he poured water from a pitcher into a basin and splashed a little onto his face. He banged on the wall that separated his room from Gid's.

"Gid. Gid, wake up. Let's get goin'," he called.

"Yeah, yeah, I'm awake," Gid's muffled voice sounded through the wall.

A few minutes later Will and Gid tromped downstairs, past the snoring hotel clerk, and out into the early morning coolness.

The difference between Black Rock in the morning and Black Rock in the evening was like that of two towns. Last night the streets had been noisy with high-pitched laughter, boisterous song, loud talk, and banging guns, most discharged in fun, a few in anger. But even the most dedicated reveler was in bed now, and the only sounds to be heard were the sounds of the other half of the town ... the working half... waking up.

There was the sound of the scrape, roll, and drop of cargo as a freight wagon was being loaded. They walked by a woman doing her wash, and Will could hear the scuffing sound of wet clothes being rubbed back and forth across a washboard. An early riser was doing some carpentry work, and Will heard the rip and tear of the saw-teeth, chewing into the piece of lumber, adding its noise to the morning cacophony.

Will woke the stable boy and paid the fare, not only for his and Gid's horses, but for Hoyt and Kellett's horses as well.

"At least the horses look ready," Gid said.

"That's good," Will replied. "I have no desire to have one of them break down on us."

The two brothers rode down to the far end of the street, leading the two empty, but saddled horses. The hollow sounding hoof beats echoed loudly off the walls of the storefronts.

"Curious, isn't it?" Will asked.

"What's curious?"

"How four horses can walk down a main street at high noon and barely be heard, and yet now the hoofbeats are so loud that I doubt we could make any more noise by banging on a drum."

They stopped in front of the sheriff's office and tied up at the hitching rail.

Inside the office, the sheriff was already up, sitting at his desk. He had a bandage tied all the way around his head, covering his shot-up ear. As a result he looked much more badly hurt than he was. He was drinking coffee and eating a biscuit, and he glared at Will and Gid.

"Good morning, Sheriff," Gid said, with exaggerated cheer. "I see you fixed breakfast."

"Not for you two, I didn't," the sheriff growled.

Gid walked over to the stove and lifted the coffee-pot, then he opened the saver and looked inside at a full pan of biscuits.

"Uhmm, that sure smells good," Gid said.

"That's for my deputies," the sheriff said.

Will clinked a half-dollar down on the corner of the sheriff's desk.

"Tell 'em to get their breakfast somewhere else," he ordered. He filled two cups, then grabbed four biscuits and started back to the cells. "Hoyt, Kellett, wake up," he called. "It's time to be goin'." He passed the coffee and biscuits through the bars.

"You poison this?" Hoyt asked.

"Now why would I poison you, Hoyt?" Will answered good naturedly. "If I didn't want to see you hang, I would've shot you last night. Besides, seein' as how you missed your supper, I figured you might be hungry this morning."

"Yeah," Hoyt said. "Yeah, that's right. I did miss my supper last night. What happened to it, anyway?"

"I ate it," Gid said, coming up to stand just outside the cell. He was eating a biscuit as well, which he devoured half of in one bite."

"The way you're wolfing that down, it's a wonder we're getting' anything at all this mornin'," Hoyt complained.

Kellett took his breakfast without comment, and the two men returned to their bunk, where they sat down to eat.

"Don't get to thinking you're having breakfast at Delmonico's," Will told them. "Swallow that down pretty quick. I'm about to have a little breakfast of my own, and when I'm done, we're leavin' whether you're finished or not."

"Where you planning on takin' us?" Kellett asked.

"Back to Bonito, where we're going to watch you die."

"Hah! You think I'm going to hang?" Kellett asked with a scoffing laugh.

"That's for the jury to decide," Will said.

"You damn right it is," Kellett said. "And the jury's

got nothing on me. I'm willin' to lay a bet, right here and now you ain't goin' to watch me hang."

Will smiled at Kellett, but the smile got no farther than the spreading of his lips and the baring of his teeth. Such a smile did nothing to soften his countenance. Instead, it made him look even more menacing. "Oh, I may not watch you hang," Will said, "but, I will watch you die."

Kellett started to ask him what he meant, but he hesitated when realization dawned on him. Will Crockett was telling him that if the court didn't sentence him to die, he, Will Crockett, would. And he would also carry out the penalty ... of that, Kellett had no doubt. He shivered, and Gid laughed.

"You know what it means, when you shiver like that, don't you?" he asked.

Kellett glared at him.

"It means, someone has just stepped on your grave."

Will walked over to the wall hook and took down the key ring.

"Crockett?" Eaton called. Will stopped and looked toward the sheriff. Eaton ran his hand through his hair, then adjusted the bandage around his head. "You two boys better keep an eye open," he said. "I heard some talk."

"What sort of talk?"

"Several of the boys got together last night," the

sheriff said. "They may be plannin' some sort of a surprise for you."

"Really? I know there's supposed to be honor among thieves and all that, but I hardly think the likes of Kansas Charley Kellett can instill such loyalty or honor among his peers. Perry Hoyt either, for that matter."

"They ain't doin' it for him or for Hoyt," the sheriff said. "It's just that they figure if they can kill you two boys and free your prisoners, it'll be a sign to all the other bounty hunters and lawmen that Black Rock should be left alone."

"Thanks for the warning," Will said.

"I'll be honest with you. If they get the job done, I ain't goin' to lose no sleep over it," Eaton said. "But bush-whackin' a man on the trail, that's goin' too far, even for me."

"Do you have any idea where this is supposed to happen?"

"No," Eaton said. "I told you all I know. The rest is up to you."

Will and Gid rode behind Hoyt and Kellett, using their proven method of securing the two prisoners by tying them together with hangman's nooses and then attaching the rope to one of their saddles. To be honest, it wasn't one-hundred percent certain that the nooses would really break their necks if either of them attempted to run. That was because the fear the nooses instilled in prisoners was great enough that no one had ever tried to escape.

They crossed a little stream, and Will watched the hooves kick up silver sprays of water as they went across.

"Hey," Kellett called. "Let's stop here for water."

"We've got enough water in our canteens," Will replied.

"The water in our canteens tastes like piss," Kellett said. "This will be good, cold water."

The swiftly running water in the stream was cool, and Will knew it would be good, and Kellett was right. The water in their canteens was tepid and sour. But if they stopped there, it might well be the last stop. That was because for some time now Will had been aware that three men were dogging them, riding parallel with them and, for the most part, staying out of sight. When he glanced over at Gid, he saw that his brother had noticed them as well. The two brothers nodded to each other, but they didn't say anything that would let their prisoners know that they knew they were being followed.

"We'll drink the water that's in our canteens," Will said.

The stream would have been a perfect spot for those who were following them to try their ambush if they were going to. Will didn't plan to give them that opportunity.

"I think my horse is going lame," Hoyt said a short while later.

"Do you?"

"Yeah, can't you see him? He's favorin' his left foreleg somethin' awful."

"What do you think, Gid? You're the one that's good with horses. Has Hoyt's horse come up lame?"

"Not that I can see," Gid said.

"Well, then you're blind," Hoyt said. "We've got to stop. We've got to stop, I tell you, and give him a rest. Maybe he's just picked up a stone or something."

"What do you think, Will?" Gid asked, quietly. "Both of them have tried to make us stop. Would you say they're trying to set up an ambush?"

"That's the way it appears to me, Little Brother," Will replied.

Will looked over to his left without being obvious about it, and saw three riders slipping through a notch in the hills, moving so quietly and expertly that only someone who was specifically looking for them would have noticed.

Ahead of them was a narrow draw. While they were in the draw they would be protected, but when they emerged from the other end they would be exposed.

"Will, there are some rocks just on the other side of the draw," Gid said, quietly. "If I was doin' the ambushin' instead of bein' ambushed, that's where I'd be waitin'."

"Yeah, that's pretty much the way I see it, too," Will replied.

As soon as they entered the draw, Will ordered them to stop.

"Stop? What for?" Hoyt replied. "If we're goin', let's go. No need to pussyfoot around about it."

"Well now, Hoyt, didn't you just tell us a while back that your horse was going lame. Here's your chance to take a look at him," Will suggested.

"Yeah, I know I said that, but I don't think it was anything," Hoyt replied. "I think he just picked up a small stone, then threw it, that's all. He's doin' fine now."

"Well, we'll stop anyway," Will said, giving a small jerk on the rope.

"All right, all right!" Hoyt complained. "But be careful with that rope, will you? You're goin' to break our necks if you don't watch out."

"No," Will said. "I'm goin' to break your neck if you don't watch out. Now, climb down."

The two prisoners climbed down, then Hoyt started to go through the motions of looking at his horse's hoof.

"Don't bother with that," Will said.

"What?"

"There's nothing wrong with your horse. You know it and I know it."

"Then why did we stop?"

"Because you are going to change shirts and hats with my brother."

"What? Why do you want to do that?"

"Because Gid has been admiring your shirt," Will said.

"You're crazy, I'm not changing shirts with your brother," Hoyt said. He started to get back onto his horse, but he was stopped when he heard the metallic click of Gid's pistol being cocked.

"Now, I'm just real disappointed," Gid said. "My brother promised me I could have your shirt and hat. And here you are trying to disappoint me."

"I'm just saying it don't make no sense, that's all," Hoyt said. Reluctantly he began peeling off his shirt, while Gid did the same.

"What about me?" Kellett asked. "Don't I get to get half-naked too?"

"Your turn will come," Will replied.

"My turn will come? My turn will come for what? What the hell has got into you?" Kellett asked.

"Don't worry about it," Will said. "I'll tell you what you need to know when you need to know it."

A moment later, with Hoyt wearing Gid's hat and shirt, he started to get back on his horse.

"No," Will said. "Ride Gid's horse for a while."

"Would you mind tellin' me just what the hell you are doin'?" Hoyt asked.

"Mount up," Will said. "You'll ride back here, with me. Gid, you ride up front with Kellett. I'll ride here with Hoyt."

"You've gone plumb loco," Hoyt mumbled as he mounted Gid's horse.

Remounted, the men rode through the long, narrow draw toward the bright wedge of light at the far end. The horses' hooves clattered loudly against the stone, and the echoes tumbling back to them made it sound as if an entire troop of cavalry were riding through instead of only four men.

It wasn't until the horses emerged from the other end that Hoyt suddenly figured out what Will was doing.

"No!" he shouted out loud. "No, don't shoot! Don't shoot!"

"Hoyt, what the hell's got into you?" Kellett hissed.

"Don't you see what this son of bitch has done?" Hoyt shouted. "He's got me wearin' his brother's duds an' ridin' his horse! Belton! Newberry! MacEwan! Don't shoot! It's me, Perry!"

One of the three bushwhackers stood about one-hundred yards up the trail. He could be seen from waist up, but only in silhouette against the bright sky.

"All right, Crockett," the would-be ambusher

shouted. "You pulled a pretty good one on us this time. But you got a long way to go, and I don't think you're goin' to get there."

The silhouette disappeared and, a moment later, Will heard the clatter of horses being ridden at a gallop.

"You think you're so damned smart," Hoyt said. "They'll just find someplace else. And this time they won't be fooled by changing shirts and horses."

"Hoyt," Will said, giving the rope one more good tug. Hoyt let out a choking sound. "You talk too damned much."

Chapter Nineteen

MacEwan lay on the top of the flat rock, looking back along the trail over which they had just come. He saw the four riders moving slowly but steadily to the North. From this distance he had no way of telling who was who, but it didn't really matter. Even if he did know, he was much too far out of range to do anything about it.

Behind him, Belton and Newberry sat resting. Belton was chewing on the root of a grass stem. Newberry had his boot off, examining a blister.

"You see 'em?" Belton asked.

"Yeah. They're 'bout a mile behind us."

"You figured out who is who yet?"

"No," MacEwan admitted. "Even if I did, there ain't no place we could set up a ambush between there and here. And I sure as hell don't plan to go out into the open to take 'em on."

"Why not? There's five of us and only two of them."

"Where do you get five?" Newberry asked. It was the first time he had spoken, as he had been too interested in the blister on his toe.

"Well you gotta count Hoyt and Kellett as bein' on our side," Belton said.

"Why? What the hell can they do? They ain't even armed."

"Well, I don't know. They can do somethin'," Belton suggested. "Get in the way so he can't get off a shot or somethin'."

"They'll get in the way, all right. They'll get themselves killed and us too," Newberry said. "If we get another chance at an ambush like before, I say we ought to do it."

"And I say we ought to just ride away," MacEwan said. "What the hell do we owe Hoyt and Kellett, anyway?"

"You heard what they said last night when we was at the jail visitin' them," Belton replied. "If we'd help 'em escape, they'd lead us to the money they got from the bank robbery in Crawford."

"Yeah, well, I heard they didn't get but a couple hundred dollars," MacEwan said.

"That ain't what they said last night," Newberry said. "Last night they said they got away with more'n two thousand dollars, and they'd give it all to us if we'd just help 'em escape."

MacEwan sighed. "All right, I'm still in," he said. "But what do we do now? I know the country from here to Bonito, and we won't get another chance like the one we just had."

"Wait, I got me an idea," Belton suggested. "Maybe there is another place."

"Where?" Newberry asked as, wincing in pain, he put his boots back on. "Because what I'd like to do is kill those two sons of bitches and get it over with."

"Well, there ain't no way they's goin' to get back to Bonito without goin' through Good Bend Crossing. And there ain't no way they're going through there without stoppin' for the night. We'll just get there ahead of them, and when they stop, we'll be waitin'."

"Yeah," Newberry said, smiling broadly. "Yeah, that's a good idea. And maybe we can have a few drinks while we wait."

To prevent any ambush on the trail, Will and Gid changed shirts and hats with Hoyt and Kellett a couple more times so that anyone watching from a distance would be thoroughly confused as to who was who. By the time they approached Good Bend Crossing, however, they were back in their proper attire.

As the four men rode toward the jail, the fact that two of them were connected by noosed rope caught the attention of many of the townspeople.

"Hey! It's Kellett!" a man shouted. "The Crockett brothers is bringin' in Kansas Charley Kellett!"

"The hell you say!"

"No, it's him, big as life! Perry Hoyt, too."

"I knew them boys wouldn't stay free long. Not with the reward as big as it is."

As the shouted news traveled from one to another, a crowd began to build, and the crowd followed the four horsemen down the street, running along on the boardwalk or hurrying through the dirt. Several young boys, using bent twigs as toy guns, shot at each other as they hurried alongside.

"Bang, bang! I'm Will Crockett. You're Kansas Charley Kellett, and you're dead! Bang, bang!"

"No, I'm Gid Crockett. I don't want to be Kellett. Kellett is gonna hang."

"So's Perry Hoyt."

"Wish they'd do it here so we could watch, don't you?"

Kellett, who couldn't help but overhear the shouted argument, stared straight ahead and licked his lips nervously.

Gid chuckled. "What's the matter, Kellett? You're looking a little peaked around the gills."

"Those kids," Kellett growled. "Somebody ought

to teach them manners."

By the time they reached the jail, a smiling Sheriff Lacy was standing on the front porch.

"Well, boys, what have you brought me?"

"Sheriff, in case you've never met these august gentlemen, the ugly one here, is Kansas Charley Kellett. The weasel-looking one is Perry Hoyt," Will said. "Can you keep 'em overnight for us?"

Gid got down first, then held the rope as Will got down. Then the two prisoners dismounted carefully.

"Be glad to keep 'em for you," Sheriff Lacy said. "Come on, you two. I got a nice, quiet cell just waitin' for you."

"Have 'em ready to go by sunup, would you, Sheriff?" Will asked. "We've got quite a ways to go with them, yet."

"They'll be ready. In the meantime, why don't you head on down to the saloon? I think Doctor Eastman, Neil, and the others are plannin' on givin' you all you can eat and drink."

"All we can eat and drink?" Gid asked, smiling. He rubbed his stomach. "Now, that's what I call a nice welcome."

When the two boys stepped into the saloon a few minutes later, Maggie was actually the first one to greet them. She slid her arm through Gid's and escorted him over to the same table where Will had played cards with

Doc and the others a few days earlier. A pitcher of beer and clean glasses were already there, and no sooner did the brothers sit down, someone brought them a plate of beans.

"We got a couple of steaks cookin', too, if you want 'em," Neil said.

"Sounds good," Gid said. "But, what are you doin' for my brother? He's probably hungry, too."

The others looked at each other then laughed. "Tell you what... I'll go back there and tell the cook to throw on another one," Neil said.

"And some more beans if you've got any," Gid added, taking a large spoonful.

In the far corner of the same saloon, Belton, Newberry, and MacEwan sat nursing their drinks.

"Look at the way them fools gather around those two," MacEwan said. "You'd think it was Abraham Lincoln sittin' there."

"Maybe it is," Belton suggested.

"What are you talkin' about, maybe it is?"

Belton looked at the other two and smiled. "Well, as I recollect, Abraham Lincoln got shot, didn't he?"

MacEwan and Newberry laughed out loud.

"Yeah," Newberry said. "Yeah, he did at that."

"Let's drink a toast to Old Abe," Belton offered and, laughing, the other two held their glasses out and joined in the toast.

Will and Gid ate and drank their fill that evening

"What about it, Will?" Doc asked. "Would you like to play some poker?"

Will shook his head. "Doc, I thank you for the invite, I truly do. It's always nice playing cards with honest gents, and I enjoyed our game the other day. But I'm beat, and we have a long way to go, yet. I think I'm going to just get the biggest bed in the quietest room in the hotel, and I'm going to sleep the sleep of the dead."

"D'ya hear that?" Belton hissed. "The son of a bitch wants to sleep like the dead."

"Well, we'll just have to see if we can help him out," Newberry replied.

"What about the other one? The big one?" MacEwan asked.

"You ever notice how much easier it is to break one stick at a time?" Belton asked. "We'll take care of the Crocketts just like that."

MacEwan made a motion with his hands as if he were breaking a stick, then he laughed out loud.

Gid and Will, waving good-bye to the others, walked over to the Crabtree Hotel. There, they got a couple of rooms overlooking the street.

"Will you gentlemen require a knock on your door to awaken you in the morning?" the desk clerk asked.

"We'll probably wake ourselves," Will said as he

signed the guest registration book. "But if you haven't seen us by sunup, give us a yell."

"Yes, sir, Mr. Crockett, it'll be my pleasure," the hotel clerk said.

Will and Gid climbed the stairs and started down the long corridor to their rooms. The corridor was well-lighted with wall-mounted gas lanterns, which heated and filled the hallway with their quiet hissing. The room, though, Will found, was dark, cool, and inviting. The window was open, and a gentle night breeze lifted the gauze curtains. Will lit the lantern alongside his bed, took his gunbelt off, then stepped up to the open window and looked out onto the dark street below. From there he could see the side of the jail and the small, barred window at the cell where Sheriff Lacy had put the prisoners. He saw no one, but it was dark inside the cell so even if someone was standing at the window, he wouldn't have been able to see them. He yawned and stretched, then went over to extinguish the lamp, and the room went dark.

"There!" Belton said. "Did you see the son of a bitch standing there in his window, just as cool as you please?"

"Yeah, I seen him," Newberry said. "You'd think he'd have better sense than to stand there like that. Why, if we'd had a rifle, we could a picked him off like shootin' a fish in a barrel."

"And if a frog had wings he wouldn't bump his ass

ever'time he jumps," Belton growled. "Come on, let's go down to the jail and have a word with Hoyt and Kellett."

The three men walked back to the rear of the saloon, then moved along behind the row of buildings toward the jail. As they walked, their nostrils were assailed by unpleasant odors, from stale beer, to privies, to garbage dumps of rotted food. These were, however, odors of such familiarity that they scarcely noticed.

"There it is," Belton said when they reached the rear of the barber shop.

The three men moved quickly across the narrow space between the barber shop and the jail, then stood up against the wall of the jail. There the shadows and darkness shielded them from view, even if someone had been walking down the street right in front of the jail.

"Hey!" Belton called. "Hey, Kellett! Hoyt! You fellas in there?"

Kellett's face appeared in the cell window. "Yeah, we're here," Kellett said. "Where've you guys been? We haven't seen you since early this mornin'?"

"I know. After the Crocketts pulled that trick on us, changin' shirts and hats with you, we didn't get another chance," Belton said. "Until now."

"Now? What are you goin' to do now?" Hoyt asked, his face joining Kellett's in the window.

"The Crocketts has took themselves a room over to

the hotel," Newberry explained. "Soon's we're sure they're good asleep, we're goin' to go over and take care of 'em."

"Why don't you just forget about both of 'em and get us out of here?" Kellett said.

"Not yet."

"What do you mean 'not yet', you bastards?" Kellett hissed. "Damnit, the Crocketts is plannin' on takin' us back to hang! Get us out of here!"

"If we get you out before we get the Crocketts, they'll both be comin' after us," MacEwan said.

"Then get us out of here and we'll help you get 'em," Kellett suggested.

"No," MacEwan replied, shaking his head. "Me an' Belton an' Newberry done talked it over. If we get you out now, someone is liable to hear the commotion and we'll lose our chance at the Crocketts. I'm tellin' you, right now is the best chance there's ever been to kill 'em."

"All right, all right," Kellett agreed. "Kill the sons of bitches. Hell, I want the bastards dead more'n anyone. But don't leave us to rot here once you get the job done."

"Don't worry, you won't be rottin' here. Once we get you out, we'll be goin' after that money you promised us."

"Yeah, don't forget the money," Kellett said.

"Listen, Kellett, just in case somethin' goes wrong, why don't you tell us where the money is?" Belton suggested.

"What do you mean, in case somethin' goes wrong?"

"You know ... if they get on to us and we have to skedaddle. We might not get another chance this good before you two boys gets hung, and if that happens, the money won't do nobody no good, 'cause you're the only one who knows where it is."

"Yeah," Newberry said. "I think Belton has got a good point. Why don't you tell us where the money is?"

"We'll show you where the money is. We ain't goin' to tell you," Kellett said. "So I guess that means you're goin' to have to get us out of here."

"All right. I was just tryin' to plan ahead, that's all," Belton said.

"When you goin' to get the Crocketts?"

"About midnight. Right now we're goin' to go back and have a few drinks to while away the time. Then, come twelve, we'll mosey on over to the hotel and do the job."

"Listen for the shots," Newberry added. "When you hear the shots, you'll know it's us, takin' care of business."

Chapter Twenty

The girl got up from the bed and walked over to a small table, where she poured water into the large porcelain basin. When she saw Newberry staring at her, she picked up the basin and went behind the dressing screen.

"What the hell did you do that for?" Newberry asked.

"There are some things a girl needs to do in private," she answered. There was a ripple of water as she dipped the washcloth into the basin.

"You ain't a girl, you're a whore," Newberry said gruffly. "And since I paid for your time, there ain't none of it private. Now take down that there screen."

There was another rippling sound of water, but the screen stayed up.

"I said, take down that there screen!" Newberry shouted, and he got out of bed and knocked the dressing screen across the room, where it hit the wall, then splintered.

The girl let out a quick shout of fear, then cringed, frightened that he was about to hit her.

"I ain't goin' to hit you," he said. "I'm just goin' to watch. Now, go on about your business."

The girl, sobbing silently in fear and embarrassment, dipped the cloth in the water and continued bathing. There was a loud knock on the door.

"Suzie! Suzie, you all right?" a man's voice called.

"Don't you worry none about the little girlie," Newberry called back. "She's just fine."

"Suzie?" the voice called again.

"Go on about your business, damnit!" Newberry shouted. "I told you the girl is just fine."

"I want to hear her voice," the man outside the door insisted.

Newberry walked over to his pants and pulled his pistol from his holster. He pointed it at the door and cocked it.

"I ain't a goin' to tell you no more," he said.

"No, don't!" Suzie shouted. "Smokey, it's all right! I'm fine."

"You sure? I thought I heard you yell," Smokey's voice called from the other side of the door.

"It's all right, really," Suzie said. "I... I knocked over the dressing screen by accident, that's all."

"All right," Smokey said reluctantly. "But you call me if you need me."

"Go on back to your drinkin', cowboy," Newberry said. "And let us get back to our business." He laughed mockingly.

"I'll... I'll be downstairs," Smokey said.

Suzie stood up.

"What are you doin'?" Newberry asked.

"I'm finished," she said.

"You're finished? That's all there is to it?"

Suzie nodded.

"Hell, what was you so private about. You didn't do nothin' but splash a little water onto yourself."

"Do you want me to bathe you?" Suzie asked.

'What?" Newberry asked, covering himself indignantly. "No! I took me a bath not no more than two, maybe three weeks ago. I done it all by myself. And if and when I need another'n, why, I'll take that one by myself, too. Fact is, whyn't you just turn your back now an' let me get dressed?"

"Whatever you say," Suzie said, waiting until she turned before she smiled at his sudden case of modesty.

Newberry was still packing his shirt tail down in his pants as he came down the stairs to join Belton and MacEwan.

"How was she?" MacEwan asked.

"You want to know how she was, you spend your own money, you cheap Scot bastard," Newberry said.

MacEwan chuckled. "Don't need to," he said. "I figure you'll pay for it, then you won't be able to keep quiet about it. Pretty soon you'll be talkin' about it so much we won't be able to get you to shut up."

"You don't say," Newberry replied. "Well, I ain't talkin' yet. What time is it?" he asked.

Belton pointed to the clock on the wall behind the bar. "Accordin' to that it's near onto midnight," he said.

"You think they're asleep yet?"

"I reckon they are. They had a hard day and figure to get up early for another hard day tomorrow. I reckon they're asleep by now."

"I wonder if they both took the same room?"

"No, they each one of 'em got their own room."

"Good, that way we can take care of 'em one at a time, 'n by the time the second hears the gunshot, the first one will already be kilt."

Newberry loosened the pistol in his holster. "Come on, let's get this over with. What do you say we pay the sons of bitches a visit?"

Newberry, Belton, and MacEwan left the saloon, then slipped quickly and quietly through the dark of night to the front of the hotel, where they stopped.

"Look around!" Belton hissed. "You see the sheriff

or one of his deputies makin' rounds?"

"I don't see nobody," MacEwan replied.

"All right, let's go in."

The lobby was lighted by only one small lamp. Therefore it was fairly dark. It was deserted as well, for the chairs and sofas that were sometimes occupied by guests were all empty. Only the night clerk was in the lobby, and he was sitting in a chair behind the desk. His chair was tipped back, his head slumped forward. His chest was rising and falling in rhythm with his snores.

MacEwan started toward the desk.

"Where you goin'?" Newberry hissed.

"To find out what room he's in," Newberry replied.

When MacEwan reached the desk, he turned the hotel register around and ran his finger down the list of occupants. He found Will Crockett's name, written in a bold, easy-to-read signature. He had rooms 202 and 209.

He hurried back to the others.

"Find 'em?" Belton asked.

"Yeah. Two-oh-two, 'n two-oh-nine. 'N that's good, 'cause that means the rooms ain't close together."

"Get your guns out, gents, and be quiet," Newberry whispered, pulling out his own pistol.

With guns drawn, they slipped through the shadows of the lobby, then started up the stairs. When they reached the top, Newberry held his finger across his lips. Here, the light was so bright they had to squint.

"Get those damned lights out!" Belton ordered, and MacEwan moved quickly down the corridor, extinguishing each lamp until the hallway was a long tunnel of darkness.

"Come on!" MacEwan hissed loudly. "That's his door down there!"

The three men moved silently through the dark hall until they were just outside the door.

"Should we break it in?" Newberry asked.

"I don't know," Belton replied. "If we don't get it the first time, he'll hear the commotion and we'll be sittin' ducks out here."

"How else we goin' to get in?" Newberry wanted to know.

"Why don't we just try the doorknob?" MacEwan suggested, turning it slowly.

"You stupid or somethin'? You think he'd be crazy enough to leave it unlocked?" Newberry asked.

The door swung open.

"Would you look at that? He didn't even lock it," Belton said, voicing the surprise of all of them.

"Go on in."

Because of the pale moonlight that fell through the open window, the room was brighter than the now-darkened hall-way. They could see the bed and Will's hat and pistol belt hanging from the brass bedpost.

"This is goin' to be like takin' candy from a baby," Belton said, aiming at the bed.

Belton fired and his shot was followed almost immediately by the other two so that, for a moment, all three guns were firing, lighting up the darkness with white flashes and filling the room with thunder.

After firing three shots apiece, Belton shouted to stop firing.

"The whole town will be in here in a minute. We got to get out of here," he said. "Check and make sure the son of a bitch is dead!"

MacEwan walked over to the bed and felt around, then gasped in surprise.

"Belton! He ain't here!" he shouted.

"What? Where is he?"

"I'm right here," Will said. He was standing on the porch roof, just outside his window.

With shouts of frustrated rage and fear, all three would-be assassins turned their guns toward the window and began firing. Bullets crashed through the window, sending large shards of glass out onto the porch roof. Will had jumped to one side of the window as soon as he spoke, and thus avoided the initial fusillade. After the first volley, Will leaned around and fired into the room. He hit one of the men and saw him go down. The other two bolted through the door.

At first Will planned to go after them by climbing back into the room, but he knew they would be leaving the hotel, so he decided to just wait until they were on the street. There, they would have fewer places to hide... and there would be less likelihood of an innocent bystander being hurt.

Will, who had been sleeping on the porch roof, fully clothed, ran to the edge of the roof, then jumped down into the space between the hotel and the building next door. He waited there in the shadows and kept his eyes on the front door of the hotel. As he expected, the door burst open a moment later and two men ran out. Will stepped out into the street to brace them.

"Hold it right there!" he called to them.

"It's Crockett!" one of the two men shouted, and he fired.

The bullet whizzed by Will's ear, much closer than was comfortable, and Will returned fire, shooting above, and just to the right of the shooter's flame pattern. He heard a grunt of pain.

The lone survivor darted across the street and disappeared into the darkness on the other side. Crouching low, Will moved back into the darkness on his side of the street, then began searching, trying to find his quarry. He saw Gid coming out of the hotel then.

"Gid, get out of the light!" Will called.

Gid moved into the shadows, then ran across the street. He squatted down beside Will. "What's goin' on?" he asked. "Did Kellett and Hoyt escape?"

"No," Will said. "But the three men who were trailing us paid me a visit."

The assailant fired from the shadows on the other side of the street, and his bullet hit the post between Gid and Will, sending pieces of wooden splinters into their faces.

"Damn, that hurt!" Gid said, pulling a splinter from his cheek.

"How'd the son of a bitch see us here?" Will asked.

"There," Gid said, pointing.

Someone in the building behind them, curious as to what was going on, had lit a lantern. It sent a golden splash of light outside, putting Will and Gid in silhouette.

"Shoot through the window," Will said. "That'll make them extinguish the lantern. But don't hit anyone."

Gid nodded, then sent a bullet through the window in the corner. It had the desired effect, for the lantern went out immediately.

As soon as Gid shot, they changed locations, which was good because, from the shadows on the other side of the road, their assailant fired at them, using the flame pattern of Gid's shot as his target.

Will shot back at the assailant's flame pattern, but he knew it was a wasted shot. The guy was pretty good, and knew to move after each shot.

Suddenly a horse burst out of the shadows from across the street, and its rider, bending low, began firing at Will and Gid.

Both Gid and Will fired back. They missed the rider, but one of them hit a lit kerosene lantern than hung on an arm sticking out over the street from the corner of the leather goods store. The bullet burst the kerosene tank and sent the fuel up into the lighted chimney, causing the lantern to explode. When it did so, it sent a shower of flaming kerosene onto the rider's back.

"Ahhhhiieee!" the rider screamed in terror and pain as he galloped down the street, flaming now like a human torch.

Will stepped out into the street and held his pistol out in front of him. He took a long, careful aim at the ball of fire, which had now panicked the running horse into galloping faster than ever. By now the outlaw was nearly one-hundred yards away.

Will squeezed the trigger and the pistol fired. At the far end of the street, the fleeing, flaming, rider pitched out of his saddle with a bullet in the back of his head, dead before he even hit the dirt. He lay there on the ground, burning for several seconds until a couple of the citizens from that end of town, having been awakened by the commotion, hurried out into the street to douse the flames.

By now Sheriff Lacy was on the scene, wearing pants, boots, and his undershirt. He hadn't even bothered to strap on his pistol, though he was carrying a rifle.

"What happened?" he asked.

"Some men tried to kill me," Will explained. "There's one up in my hotel room, and another across the street." He pointed to a body, close by in the street. That body, like the one at the far end of the street, was already drawing a crowd.

"Are they locals?" the sheriff asked in surprise.

Will shook his head. "I don't think so. I think these were the same men we saw dogging us on the trail today. I was pretty sure they might try again tonight, so I was ready for them."

Sheriff Lacy shook his head and chuckled. "Ready for them, huh? I guess you were."

Chapter Twenty-One

Good Bend Crossing had telegraphed ahead the news that Will and Gid Crockett would be arriving with Perry Hoyt and Kansas Charley Kellett. So when the three men rode into Bonito, the entire town was turned out to meet them.

"Did they give you boys much of a fight?" someone called.

"Hey, Kansas Charley, you think you'll get away this time?"

"I'll be comin' to your dance, Kellett!"

Kellett stared ahead glumly, and when they reached the jail, Sheriff McIvor and Judge Fowler were standing there on the porch to meet them.

"Well, Kellett, I've been wanting to have you as my guest for a long, long time," Sheriff McIvor said.

"You go to hell," Kellett snarled.

"Now, that's no way to be," McIvor said.

"I hope you got somethin' to eat in there," Hoyt said. "We ain't et nothin' but jerky for three days, now." Hoyt started toward the front door of the jailhouse, but Sheriff McIvor reached out his hand to stop him.

"Huh uh, Perry, you won't be goin' in there," he said.

"What do you mean?"

"Boys, take him over to the courtyard and put him in the holding cell."

"The holding cell?" Hoyt said in dread. "No! What are you goin' to put me there for?"

"Why, Mr. Hoyt, don't you remember?" McIvor said. "That's where you were headed when you escaped."

"Yeah, but you don't go there until just before you hang. What is this, a lynchin'? Don't I even get a trial first?"

"You've had your trial," Judge Fowler replied. "There's no need to try you again. You were found guilty, you were sentenced to hang, and hang you shall, this very afternoon."

"No! Kellett, do somethin'," Hoyt shouted as a couple of deputies led him toward the courthouse. "They're fixin' to hang me!"

"Quit your belly achin', Hoyt, an' take your hangin' like a man," Kellett said.

"Is that all you got to say?" Hoyt asked.

"Ain't my problem," Kellett said. "I ain't the one hangin' this afternoon. You are."

"You son of bitch! I'll see you in hell!" Hoyt shouted as they took him away.

Kellett began to laugh.

"I don't know what you have to laugh about, Kellett," Sheriff McIvor said. "I figure we'll have you tried tomorrow mornin' and hung by tomorrow afternoon."

"Yeah? Well, I ain't got no rope around my neck yet. And you can ask these here Missouri pukes, I ain't that easy to hold on to. Tell him, Crockett. Tell him!" Kellett said, with a mocking laugh.

"Kellett, I'm going to enjoy watching you hang. And if the sheriff's arm is sore, I'll even pull the handle myself," Will said.

"I'll have the money ready for you two boys this afternoon," Judge Fowler said.

"Money?" Kellett said. He looked at Will and Gid. "I thought this was somethin' personal between us, somethin' from the war. Didn't know you was gettin' blood money."

"It is personal," Gid said. "And knowing it's money for your blood makes it even sweeter."

"We'll be around this afternoon, Judge," Will said. "But first we're going to take a bath, get a good, hot meal, then a hotel room. If we're going to wait around to see Kellett hang, we may as well wait in comfort."

"You son of a bitch! You'll never see me hang!"

Kellett said.

"Get him inside," Judge Fowler ordered, and Sheriff McIvor and the remaining deputy escorted Kellett into the jail.

By two o'clock in the afternoon, both Crocketts were bathed, wearing clean clothes, and standing in Judge Fowler's office.

"I've got the money right here for you boys," Judge Fowler said, taking it out of his desk drawer. "The reward I promised you for Kellett plus the reward that was already posted for the others. And I must tell you, I have never paid out a reward with more pleasure. That is one bunch of men I am glad to see gone. He counted the money, then held it out. "Who gets it?"

"Give it to Gid," Will said. "He's the one that keeps up with our money."

"Thanks," Gid said, taking the money. "What time will Kellett's trial be tomorrow?"

"Nine in the morning," Judge Fowler answered. "We'll find him guilty by eleven, feed him his last meal at twelve, and hang him at two."

"We'll be there."

Judge Fowler stroked his chin. "You know, you got paid the same for all of them. But I get the distinct feeling you got more satisfaction from bringing him in than all the others put together."

"That's right," Will said.

"Why? Because of the girl? You knew her, didn't you?"

"Yes. We knew her. Her mother was a relative of ours, and her father once rode with us."

"Rode with you? Oh, you mean during the war?"

"Yes."

"Wait a minute, Kellett was a Jayhawker, wasn't he? And you boys were with Quantrill, I believe? Yes, I can see where there might be bad blood between you."

"The bad blood started even before we joined Quantrill," Gid said.

"Oh? How can that be?"

Gid told about finding their house burned and their parents murdered.

"The head of that band of murdering bastards was a man named Otto Hoffman. And what they did had nothing to do with the war."

The sheriff nodded toward the back of the jail. "And Kellett? What was his role in that?"

"Kellett rode with Hoffman. That's enough," Gid said.

"I see. Then that would make it worse. Well, I not only congratulate you boys for bringing him in, I commend you for not letting your personal feelings get in the way. I know you were tempted to kill Kellett yourself, and, under the circumstances, if you had done it, you would probably have gotten away with it. I admire your respect for the law."

Will smiled. "Respect for the law has nothing to do with it," he said. "I never met anyone yet who wouldn't rather be shot than hanged."

There was a knock on the door and Judge Fowler yelled for whoever it was to come in. It was his law clerk.

"Judge," the clerk said. "They've got Perry Hoyt standing out on the gallows. The sheriff is waiting for your signal."

"Yes," Judge Fowler said. He sighed and looked up at Will. "You know I can sentence someone to die, and in the case of a person like Perry Hoyt, a cold blooded murderer, I can do it with a clear conscience. But when it comes to the part where I actually have to give the signal to dispatch the soul of another human being into eternity, I must confess to having qualms." He walked over to the window. "Come, watch with me," he said. "After all, you have a hand in this, too."

Will and Gid walked over to the window and looked down into the courtyard below. There were three or four-hundred people gathered around the gallows. There were reporters and a photographer in the front row. Although Hoyt had just been brought in that same morning, the reporters were local only, there being insufficient time to gather any from the national newspapers.

Hoyt was standing just under the crossbeam with the noose around his neck and a hood over his face. His hands were manacled to his belt, so that his arms were stiffly by his sides. His legs were tied together. Any last words he may have had were already spoken at that point, and he was quietly counting off the last seconds of his life.

Judge Fowler nodded his head, and down on the gallows, Sheriff McIvor, who had been awaiting the signal, pulled the handle. From his position at the open window in Judge Fowler's office, Will and Gid could hear the thump of the dropping trapdoor, then the oohs and ahs of the assembled crowd. Perry Hoyt dropped straight and true, made one half turn to the left, then was very still.

Though the sun was a full disk up in the Eastern sky, Will was still sound asleep. He was awakened by a loud banging on his hotel room door. He sat up quickly, drawing his gun from the holster, which hung on the bedstead.

"What is it?" he shouted gruffly.

"Crockett, it's me, Sheriff McIvor. Open up."

Still holding his gun, Will walked over to the door and opened it slightly, just to make certain the sheriff was alone. When he saw that he was alone, he opened it all the way.

"Yeah, come on in," he said invitingly. He took

his pants off the back of the chair and started putting them on.

As he did so, he saw the look of agitation on the sheriff's face. "Is it Kellett?" he asked.

"Yes. How did you know?"

"Just a hunch."

"When I came to the office this morning, I found my night deputy lying dead, just outside the cell. His throat had been cut. Evidently Kellett had lured him over to the cell on some pretense, then managed to cut his throat and get the keys."

Gid came out into the hallway from his own room, still tucking his shirt into his trousers. "You say the deputy's throat was cut?" Gid asked.

"Yes. He bled to death on the floor of the jail. My God, you should see the blood."

"How did Kellett get a knife?" Gid asked. "I know for a fact, he didn't have one when we brought him in."

"Well, that's the damndest thing," McIvor said. "He took a piece from the bed and made himself a knife."

"You seem to have a hell of a time holding on to your prisoners, Sheriff," Will challenged.

"I can't deny that," the sheriff said contritely.

"Have you looked around your office? What's missing?" Will asked.

"A rifle, pistol and holster, and two or three boxes

of ammunition. It looks like he also took the deputy's horse, so he's well armed and well mounted."

By now Will had on his boots and was strapping on his gun. "So are we," he said.

"Then you boys are going after him? That's a relief, I was hoping you'd say that. You'll bring him back?"

"You asked two questions, Sheriff," Will replied. "And I'm only going to answer the first one. Yes, we are going after him."

Chapter Twenty-Two

The Crocketts were able to follow Kellett because the deputy's horse he was riding was a town horse. As a town horse, his food consisted primarily of oats. That made his droppings very distinctive.

Gid, who was the better tracker of the two, was dismounted, reading a sign. Will, who was still in the saddle, took a swallow of water from his canteen, ran the back of his hand across his lips, then replaced the canteen.

"What do you think, Little Brother?" he asked.

Gid stood up, then looked toward the South. "You know, at first I thought Kellett would be heading for Black Rock, but I think he has something else in mind."

"What?"

"I think he's heading for Mexico."

"Damn," Will said. "And he's got what? A three-hour head start on us?"

2322223223222222

"Doesn't matter," Gid said. "The way he's pushing, he'll kill his horse long before he reaches the border."

Though it was difficult to keep themselves in check, Will and Gid rode easily, sparingly, knowing that in the long run they would make just as good time because their animals would still be fresh, while Kellett's horse would be wearing out.

On the third day, they got close enough to get a glimpse of Kellett in the distance. That was when they knew he was heading for Hachita, another one of the little towns on the American side of the border.

The boys arrived in Hachita at just about supper time, and, along with the spicy aromas of Mexican cooking, they could smell coffee, pork chops, fried potatoes, and baking bread.

"Rosina? Rosina?" a woman called, and Gid, startled because the woman was very close to him, jerked his horse to a halt to look in the direction of the call.

"Si, Senora?" a young Mexican girl answered.

"Take the clothes down from the line, will you?" the woman ordered.

"Si, Senora," the girl replied.

The woman looked at Gid nervously and took a step backwards. Gid touched the brim of his hat in greeting, then urged his horse on.

In front of the feed store, two gray-bearded men

JUDGEMENT DAY

were engaged in a game of checkers, watched over by a half-dozen kibitzers. A couple of them looked up as Will and Gid rode by, their horses' hooves clattering loudly on the hard-packed street. Neither of the kibitzers seemed to recognize them. That was good, because they didn't exactly want their presence announced.

The shopkeeper of the dry goods store stepped through his front door and began vigorously sweeping the wooden porch. His broom did little but cause the dust to swirl about, then fall back down again. He brushed a sleeping dog off the porch, but even before the shopkeeper was back inside, the dog reclaimed his position, curled around comfortably, and, within a moment was asleep again.

Gid saw the horse from the far end of the street. As he had known from the trail, the horse had been ridden nearly to death, and even from there he could see that the animal was totally defeated.

"There's his horse," Gid said, pointing to the horse. "Anyone who would treat an animal like that should be horsewhipped."

The two brothers rode slowly down to the far end of the street, then tied their horses to a hitch rail next to the poor animal. Gid walked over to the horse and patted it on the neck. The horse's coat was smeared with foam and it was breathing in labored gasps. Its muzzle and the

233

hitch rail were flecked with blood, which had spewed from its mouth and nostrils by the painful breaths.

"Oh, Jesus," Gid said. He looked at Will with an expression of sorrow and outrage on his face. "Look at the blood. The poor critter's lungs have burst."

"What can be done for it?" Will asked.

Gid shook his head. "Nothing. He's in unbearable pain." Sighing, Gid pulled his pistol and aimed it at the horse's head. The horse looked toward him, his big brown eyes sad and knowing. He nodded once, almost as if telling Gid that he understood what had to be done. The horse looked away then and waited stoically for the release from its suffering. Gid pulled the trigger and the horse fell to the ground. The gunshot echoed through the quiet streets for a long time. Then it was silent.

The gunshot attracted several of the townspeople, and they looked toward the saloon at the two men, one with a smoking gun, and at the horse lying motionless on the street. A curtain fluttered in one of the false fronts. A cat yowled somewhere down the street. A fly buzzed past Gid's ear, did a few circles, then descended quickly to the horse, joined almost immediately by a dozen others, drawn to the unexpected feast.

Leaving Gid out front, Will pushed through the batwing doors, then stepped to one side, with a wall at his back. At the bar, a glass of beer in front of him, his lips dripping with moisture, stood Kansas Charley Kellett.

Will's lips twisted into an evil smile. Part of him wanted to kill the man that instant, while part of him wanted to delay his pleasure. He remembered the fear Perry Hoyt had shown toward hanging, and he wanted Kellett to know that same terror. Maybe he would take him back.

"Kellett," Will said. His words were cold, flat, menacing.

Kellett didn't turn around, didn't even look at him in the mirror. Instead, he stared into his glass of beer with those cold, droopy eyes.

"Well, look who's here. I would've thought you'd give up on me by now."

"I've come for you, Kellett."

There were a half-dozen drinkers at the bar, and at Will's words, they hurried to get away. Tables and chairs scooted across the floor as everyone in the saloon got up and moved back against the wall, out of the line of fire.

Will caught the movement of the others out of the corner of his eye. He was pretty sure Kellett had not picked up any partners in his short flight of freedom, but he wanted to be certain. A quick glance was all it took to convince him that there was no one else who represented any danger to him.

Kellett still did not turn around. "What was that

shooting out front?" he asked.

"My brother shot your horse."

"He shouldn't have done that. That was a good horse."

"Not after you got through with him, you horse-kill-ing son of a bitch. You rode him until his lungs burst."

"Son of a bitch, did you hear that?" one of the saloon patrons asked.

"That's no way to treat a horse," another said.

Kellett paid no attention to the comments. "Well, he wasn't my horse, anyway," Kellett said. "As you know, I just borrowed him when I left," Kellett said with a low, evil laugh.

"You disappointed a few folks back there, Kellett. They were wanting to see you dance."

"Did I? Well, I thought I'd just let Mr. Hoyt do the dancing for both of us."

"Hoyt did his show. Now it's your turn."

"No thank you. I got no plans to go hang."

"I don't give a damn what your plans are, Kellett. You're going back, and you're going to hang."

"If you're so all fired set on seein' me dead, Crockett, why don't you just shoot me here and be done with it?"

"No way" Will said. "Shooting is too good for you. I saw the way Hoyt sweated before he was hanged. I don't intend to deny myself the pleasure of seeing you go through the same thing."

Kellett turned away from the bar to look at Will. He was smiling evilly.

"You know, Crockett, I wondered why you and your brother was doggin' me like you been doin'. Then someone told me that you took it real personal what me and Alvarado did to that young Patton girl." He rubbed himself. "She was young, but she was fine. Just real fine."

A blood vessel in Will's temple began to work, and his eyes narrowed.

Seeing that his words were having some effect on him, Kellett continued. "They said you was some kin to her. Is that right?"

"That's right," Will said.

"That why you and your brother dogged me so hard?"

"That's why."

Kellett's evil smile spread. "Well, then maybe I got somethin' here that'll square things up between us. Somethin' that belonged to that little ol' girl. If you want, you can keep it as a little memento." He started to reach into his vest pocket.

"Don't do it, Kellett!" Will cautioned.

Kellett held out his hand. "Hey, now, hold on there," he said. "I ain't goin' for no gun. Like I told you, all I'm reachin' for is a little memento." His hand came back out of his pocket, clutching a little piece of brown leather. "See?" He held it out toward Will. "This here's for you. You and your brother. I'm givin' it to you."

"What is it?" Will asked, trying to study it from where he stood.

Kellett's evil grin grew wider. "Hell, I thought you said you knowed her, Crockett. What's the matter? Didn't you ever see that little girl's titties? This here is one of her titties. The left one. It ain't very big, but then, she wasn't a woman full grow'd yet. She had titties, but they was little things."

Suddenly a picture flashed in Will's mind. He could recall vividly the scene of her mutilated body and the missing left breast. He realized at that moment that Kellett was telling the truth.

"You sorry son of a bitch," he swore.

"Here, take it!" Kellett suddenly shouted, tossing it toward Will.

Will's first reaction was of revulsion, then he saw that Kellett was using that as a diversionary tactic, for in the same motion of the toss, his hand snaked down to his side to draw his pistol.

Will reacted to the sudden move quickly, drawing his own pistol faster than he had ever drawn it before, spurred on in the effort by years of controlled rage toward this man, the rage highlighted by his latest atrocity. He had his own gun out in time to take quick but deliberate aim and shoot Kellett in the gut. Kellett, the barrel of his own pistol just topping the holster, pulled the trigger, shooting lead into the floor. A red stain began to spread just over his belt buckle.

Kellett's gun clattered to the floor, and he put his hands over his belly wound and watched the blood spill through his fingers. Inexplicably, he smiled.

"You're fast, Crockett," he said. "Faster'n I thought." He weaved back and forth for a moment, then pitched forward, crashing through a table before landing on the floor.

Smoke from the discharge of the two weapons formed a big cloud, then began to drift toward the ceiling.

"Will!" Gid shouted, coming inside at the sound of the gunshots.

"I'm all right, Little Brother," Will answered, holding his hand out toward Gid. Gid, who had drawn his pistol, looked down at Kellett. Seeing that Kellett represented no danger to either of them, Gid put his gun away.

Will knelt beside Kellett. Kellett, who was still alive, struggled to sit up. Will helped him, then leaned him back against the bar. Kellett looked at Will and smiled. As he did so, a trickle of blood ran from his mouth ... evidence that the bullet had pierced his lung. Every breath was painful to him, and it was evident in his face as he breathed.

ROBERT VAUGHAN

"Well, I reckon you've killed me," he said.

"This isn't how I wanted you to die, Kellett," Will replied. "I wanted to take you back. I wanted to see you hang."

Kellett tried to laugh, but it came out in a barking cough. Little flecks of blood sprayed out on his lips and on his shirt.

"When you think about it, I reckon I beat you after all," he rasped. "I told you I wasn't goin' to hang, and as you can see, I ain't."

"I guess you're right," Will said. He stood up and rammed his pistol back in his holster. "But dead's dead, I reckon."

The bat-wing doors swung open and a man with a badge came inside. His hair and mustache were gray, his face lined around his blue eyes. There was a sharpness to his eyes that told Will the peace officer had probably been pretty good when he was younger. Only age had driven him to a backwater place like Hachita, where little happened. Age had undoubtedly slowed him down, but Will imagined there were still a few who could make the mistake of misjudging him. Will didn't intend to make that mistake.

"You shoot this fella?" the man with the badge asked, nodding toward Kellett, who was leaning back against the bar.

"Yes," Will answered.

"Want to tell me what it's all about?"

Kellett tried to laugh, another coughing, blood-spraying laugh. "Sheriff, don't blame my friend here," he said. "If he hadn't killed me, I would have killed him. Fact is, he done me a favor. This way, at least, I ain't goin' to hang."

"That's right, Sheriff," one of the witnesses said. "The fella on the floor drew first. It was a pure case of self-defense."

"You shoulda seen it, Sheriff," another offered. "It was the fastest thing I ever seen in my life."

The sheriff looked at Will, then at Gid. "Are you two together?"

"We're brothers," Gid said.

"Did you team up on this man?"

"We tracked him here," Will said. "But when the shooting came, it was just Kellett and me."

"Kellett?" the sheriff asked in surprise, looking down at the man against the bar.

"Kansas Charley Kellett," Will said.

"I'll be damned."

"You heard of me, Sheriff?" Kellett choked. "You read any of the novels about me?"

"I've heard about you," the sheriff replied. "But what I read about you ain't been novels."

"I'm famous," Kellett said. "People in New York City have read about my exploits," he added.

"Did you have to bring your beef to my town?" the sheriff asked Will.

"Sorry, Sheriff, but this is where we caught up with him," Will replied.

"You two boys bounty hunters?"

"Not really," Will said. "Though we intend to claim the reward on his miserable hide."

"Why, Sheriff, I can't believe you don't know who these men are," Kellett said. "These here boys are the Crockett brothers."

The crowd reacted audibly to Kellett's announcement.

"The Crocketts?" someone said.

"The Crocketts, Will and Gid," another said.

"I've heard of 'em."

"Boys we're goin' to have some story to tell. We just seen the Crocketts in action," another said.

The sheriff held up his hand to still the crowd reaction.

"I've heard of you, boys," he said. "Far as I know, you aren't wanted men, but they say you're a couple of hard cases. I've never heard-tell of either one of you killing anyone who didn't need killing. But if there's anything I don't want in this town it's a couple of gunfighters, even if there's no paper out on you. Do you understand?"

"We'll be on our way, Sheriff, soon as you give us a receipt that says we turned Kellett over to you."

The sheriff went over to the bar. "Slim, you got a tablet and pencil?"

The bartender reached under the bar then came up with the items.

"You really are Charles Kellett, like he says?" the sheriff asked Kellett.

"That's it, Sheriff. Charles Kellett, with two t's," Kellett said. "I don't want my name misspelled when they write the story."

"Received of Will and Gid Crockett, the body of one Charles Kellett, wanted man, killed in a fair gunfight in the town of Hachita. Signed, Sheriff Herbert Miller," the sheriff said, speaking aloud as he wrote.

Kellett laughed weakly.

"What are you laughing at, Kellett?"

"The way you're givin' a receipt for me ... sayin' I was killed in a gunfight, when I ain't even dead yet."

"You're dead, Kellett," the sheriff said easily. "You just ain't laid down yet." He tore the page off the tablet and handed it to Will. "Will this do for you?" he asked.

"That will do just fine, Sheriff. Thank you," Will answered, folding the piece of paper and putting it in his shirt pocket. "Come on, Gid. Let's go."

The two men started toward the door.

"Crockett, wait a minute!" Kellett called to Will. "You ain't goin' to just leave me like this, are you? I got a pain in my gut somethin' awful. Why didn't you shoot me in the head or the heart and get it over with?"

"I shot you just where I wanted to shoot you, Kellett," Will said.

"Well finish me off now, you bastard!" Kellett shouted. "Don't you leave me like this!"

Will started for the door again.

"Crockett! Crockett! Don't forget the girl's tit!" Kellett called. "You wouldn't want to leave her little tittie behind for someone else to play with, would you?"

Will stopped.

"Yeah!" Kellett said, seeing Will weaken. "Yeah, think about that little tittie. I cut it offen her, Crockett. And she wasn't dead yet, neither. She screamed like a stuck pig when I cut it offen her."

Will remained rooted to the floor, though his hand began to move slowly toward his pistol.

"That's it!" Kellett said. "That's it! Shoot me! Yes, go ahead! Shoot me!"

Will sighed and let his arm drop down to his side. He started once more toward the door.

"Don't you want me to die? What's the matter? Are you showing yellow?"

Will and Gid pushed through the bat-wing doors, walked by Kellett's dead horse, then climbed on their own horses for the long ride back to Bonito. Behind them, they could hear Kellett's screams of rage and pain. It was like music to their ears.

A Look At: A Time To Die
(The Crocketts' Western Saga: Eight)

Join the Crockett brothers' adventures through the western frontier.

Attacked and left for dead, Win Coulter drags himself into Horseshoe, Nevada, to lick his wounds. When a no-good sheriff gets in his way, Win gets a date with the gallows. But you can't count one Coulter out when his brother has the gumption – and the guns – to do something about it.

AVAILABLE NOVEMBER 2021

About the Author

Robert Vaughan sold his first book when he was 19. That was 57 years and nearly 500 books ago. He wrote the novelization for the mini-series Andersonville. Vaughan wrote, produced, and appeared in the History Channel documentary Vietnam Homecoming.

His books have hit the NYT bestseller list seven times. He has won the Spur Award, the PORGIE Award (Best Paperback Original), the Western Fictioneers Lifetime Achievement Award, received the Readwest President's Award for Excellence in Western Fiction, is a member of the American Writers Hall of Fame and is a Pulitzer Prize nominee.

Vaughan is also a retired army officer, helicopter pilot with three tours in Vietnam. And received the Distinguished Flying Cross, the Purple Heart, The Bronze Star with three oak leaf clusters, the Air Medal for valor with 35 oak leaf clusters, the Army Commendation Medal, the Meritorious Service Medal, and the Vietnamese Cross of Gallantry.

CPSIA information can be obtained
at www.ICGtesting.com
Printed in the USA
LVHW041641131021
700348LV00014B/395

9 781647 347857